Some readers' comments of earlier stories by Ian Burns

The Wisdom of Harkishen Singh   What a wonderfully innovative publication! I think it ranks as only one of its kind, a glorious tribute to a country from someone from another, a great juxtaposition of the visual, poesy and profundity.   Moola Bhaktavatsala, Bangalore, India

Ranga Plays Australia   The book is a delight.   Lindsay Armstrong, New Gisborne

Ranga Plays Australia   Funny, interesting and not too hard to read and understand, which was nice.   Anuj Kumar, London

Ranga Plays Australia   To me it is one of the best books I have read that initiates a child into an alien country while at the same time working as a text of study.   Moola Bhaktavatsala, Bangalore

Ranga Plays Australia   It feels thoroughly researched and demonstrates a great love and understanding of cricket. There is a subtle humour, throughout the text, that caused this reader to chuckle more than once.   The Historical Novel Society

Ranga Plays Australia   Well all up the best part of the story I would think was the end. It was a fantastic end to a fantastic story.   Ashleigh, Greensborough

Ranga Plays Australia   This delightful story comes with a sparkle of freshness and simplicity and the reader will be left wondering how much is fact and how much is the imagination of the author.   Neil Thompson, Diamond Creek

Ranga Plays Australia   [The author's] description of Ranga in an Indian village environment is really astonishing.   S. K. Bandyopadhyay, Bangalore

Messing With Your Mind This is a very culturally diverse and uniquely Australian Novel. Both a collection of short stories with their own unique set of events and an overriding mystery that carries you through to a surprising end.   Matthew Hughes-Gage, Melbourne

The Alone Man This is one of the most beautiful stories I can say that I have read in a long time and it brought tears to my eyes. Carolyn Jacobsen, Tura Beach, NSW
The Alone Man I thoroughly enjoyed this short story. It's poetic, informative and Australian. Matthew Hughes-Gage, Melbourne

The Package on the Tram Colour-changing cobwebs,..... impossible? A detective working with seven puppies....... unlikely? A dog as large as a mammoth.......crazy? Getting lost in a forest of animal fur......yeah?? A fine read for children and grandchildren. And you will enjoy it also. Gysbert Fine, Eltham

Scratcher I found Scratcher a very funny, unique and exciting book. Sahaj, Bangalore, India
Scratcher I'D EASILY GIVE IT A BIG 10 out of 10! Matt, South Frankston

The Search for Quong I would recommend the book to other kids. It's got all funny names for animals and other creatures. Rebecca Kreltzsheim, Wangaratta

Twevven and the big, bigger biggest baby burp This is a delightful read and will be one of those books kids will want adults to read to them over and over. Peter Eerden, amazon.com
Twevven and the big, bigger biggest baby burp I liked when the baby farted. Favian, Mitcham

Stories from Somewhere

An Anthology 1984-2018

Ian Burns

Copyright Ian B G Burns 2018

National Library of Australia Cataloguing-in-Publication entry:

Creator: Burns, Ian, 1939- author.

Title: Stories from Somewhere

ISBN: (paperback) 978-06483597-0-8

This is a work of fiction.

Cover design: Sophie Sirninger Rankin

Web: http://www.lulu.com/spotlight/ianburns

http://www.twevven.com

Email: ibgburns@gmail.com

The Stories

The Alone Man

He was old. Not very old, or as old as some people. But he *was* old.

Once it had been different. He'd lived there on the edge of the great red gum forest, well out of town, with his farm stretching out and down in front of him, to the river.

Fences—post-and-rail—kept the sheep in one great paddock or another, while windmills clacked up water for the paddocks away from the river, up the hill.

It'd taken years, clearing trees and scrub, burning off, ploughing through tangled roots with the old horse plodding around the stumps, and then sowing the seed.

All year round the sun shone, burning his skin first red, then brown, then like the tough, corrugated skin of the ironbark tree.

And the sun burnt the grass and the wheat, and the backs of the tough little sheep after they'd been shorn. And the chooks scratched around in the dry dust, beaks open, wings stretched out a little to trap a piece or two of dry air to cool their bodies for a second.

He'd camped in a tent. Stringybark poles held it up, and his great enamel mug hung from a nail driven into the front pole—the doorway—when it wasn't filled with steaming black tea.

Slowly, slowly, the bush turned into a farm. He built his first dam, between two sloping hills over near the road, and it half filled that winter when it hardly rained anywhere else, and overflowed in the three-day storm the next summer.

Sitting in front of his tent, in the canvas chair,

watching the shadows slip up the hill towards him, he knew he was happy.

Not many people came out that way–it was still on the edge of things–but he didn't mind.

Sometimes an old swaggie would camp a night or two with him, or someone down on his luck. They'd squat beside the embering fire, watching the little flicks of flame while their dampers cooked on the hot clay beneath them

Those nights seemed to have something special about them, even though they didn't ever talk very much. It was good just to sit near another person, to kick the coals and watch the sparks flash up to join the stars a stone's throw above his head.

The men never stayed long–a day or two at the most–and they always carried their own things. Of course they didn't mind having a bit of your sugar, as long as you had some of their tea. He'd hear about the big towns, and the gold that was being found down the track, and once a man told him tales of California and the sea to Australia.

He noticed that when it was time to turn in they'd unroll their swags down the hill from his tent, in their own space, leaving him to himself for the night–he imagined it was because they snored, although it could've been because they wanted to be on their own.

Once a week he'd saddle the horse and ride her into the little town.

He left camp when the sun was just up, not bothering with breakfast, and arrived in town two or three hours later, depending on whether the river was up or not.

Like the swaggies, he didn't stay long. He'd go into the cool general store and buy flour and sugar, tea and salt, sometimes a bit of bran or pollard for the chooks, and not much else. He hadn't the money for other things, anyway, and he didn't really need them.

Even though he only stayed there a while, he quite liked the town, especially the wide verandahs on the two or three shops, and the huge red gum beside the farrier's, with its great knotty warts.

Everybody knew him, and he knew almost everyone.

But it was good to get on the road again, before the sun was up too high, his horse's nose pointing to the low hills in the distance.

His twenty-first birthday fell on a Tuesday, and he cooked damper, filled with currants and a sprinkling of sugar on top. He wondered what the Queen was eating, on her throne, and thought that she was probably missing out. Or was it the King?

And so the first years passed by.

One day he began building a house.

Nobody knew that he was doing it, or so he thought.

It was up against the forest, close to his tent, but with a better view of the river and the far plains. He wasn't sure why he started to build the house: it just seemed the right thing to do—it needed to be done.

Everything he wanted came from the forest, except for the windows. Straight young trees not much older than he was became the corner posts, and framed the two doors. Another, stronger than the rest, lay across the top, to hold the roof. Others, roughly cut, but good, were the rafters. The walls were lengths of red gum sawn over many weeks, roundish on the outside and flat inside.

Scraping carefully with the hoe he made the floor as flat as a table, and packed the earth down with his heavy boots and a sprinkling of water. Some pieces of split timber and rope made the doors, and old wheat sacks became window shutters.

The chimney came from the river, as well as the stones for the fire.

The hardest part was the roof. He'd never cut wooden shingles before, and he made many mistakes before he had enough to keep the rain out.

It was different, coming back to a house. He felt older, more responsible. More *there*. He brought over his canvas chair and the other things, but left the tent in its spot. He liked to sit and look at it when he'd finished work, watching it puff and billow in the warm breeze, as though it was breathing.

Then he'd think—about building another dam in the top paddock, about making a proper loading pen, about a shearing shed, and a well, and, one day, an orchard; and he'd listen to the summer thunder or watch the sloping winter rain.

The bush was pushed back, away from his land, fenced off, and beaten.

He had a farm.

She was from the outback, from out past Wilcannia.

The dry land was in her eyes and in her smile, and a horse was her slave. And he found that he had to go into town nearly every day.

One day it was to get the flour he'd forgotten, another it was for some big iron nails, another . . . some twine. And his horse needed shoeing, and it was time to get the seed for next season's wheat crop, and he had to lend a hand when they started to build the church.

He was glad that no one noticed.

He had few words, and those he had were usually for men, or for buying things that hardly mattered any more.

He was rough, and awkward, and too tall; and there was always dirt under his finger nails.

But she saw with more than her eyes, and heard with more than her ears.

And before the church was finished they married, standing with the town on a dirt floor, before a rough wooden cross held together by twine and a gentle miracle.

She loved the house. He'd thought that she wouldn't, but she did.

She climbed down from the sulky and walked all around it, slowly, looking at the way he'd cut the timber, at the clever window joints, and she admired the roof shingles for a long time.

He pretended to attend to the horse, fiddling clumsily with his expert fingers, while he watched her walk and stop and gaze. How had he been so happy before?

When she reached the front her gaze left his house— *their* house—and turned over the farm: the paddocks greening in the autumn rains she'd so seldom seen; the dam, two native ducks brown specks of fluff on its surface; the river, quiet under the spreading red gums; and the hazy plain across which she'd bumped to this man.

Her arms went around his neck as he lifted her, like a child, and carried her inside.

They'd only had one wedding present, and that was one more than they'd expected.

It was from the whole town, as well as the farms beyond. And it was the only thing they really needed, because he'd forgotten all about it.

A bed.

A great bed, with brass knobs and brass bed heads, and a firm wire base. And a feather mattress and two feather pillows!

His face went as red as the sunset when he saw it, while she looked at her feet, little pleased patches of pink colouring her cheeks.

Everybody laughed and clapped their hands as they crowded round to admire it—the whole town had come out—and he looked at them all, knowing that none of them had a bed as good as this one. Her hand was in his.

The bed seemed to fill the house but then other things began to 'fit' in. He made her a dresser, with cupboards and drawers, for the china that began to appear, and the cutlery. He made a new table, cut from a native pine growing down near the river; and he made a strong chest for her clothes.

She found some wool and crocheted a bedspread,

splashes of rainbow in the gloom, and she found, almost every day, wildflowers in the forest for the windowsills.

He realised that his house was different now.

It was a *home*.

Before she'd come out to the farm he hadn't thought much about work—it just happened.

His mind somehow knew what a farm should look like and, while the sun was up and there was light somewhere in the sky, his arms and legs and body did what his mind wanted them to do.

Before she'd come out to his farm he'd taken each day as it'd come, always feeding the chooks, but then going fence-building or dam-digging, or cutting fire-wood, or even lying all day beside the river, fishing for cod or perch.

Before she'd come out to their farm it hadn't seemed to matter much about tomorrow or next year, as long as things were getting better.

That was *before*.

His mind still knew what a farm should look like, but it wasn't quite so sharp—it didn't matter quite so much if a fence-line wasn't as straight as a man could get it: it was all right if it curved around a tree or a granite boulder that *she* loved.

Each night, after a meal that still made his mouth water all these years later, they'd sit in front of the fire and talk about the next day, or the next season. She knew the farm as well as he knew her face, and when they looked at each other in the firelight it was almost as though they were looking into the future.

Their minds came together as they planned the farm, little plans and big plans, though they didn't talk much about the big plans, for some reason; and one or two things they didn't talk about at all.

His breakfasts changed, too, from a slab of bread and dripping and a mug of tea, to a bowl of porridge and a fried egg on bread, or a boiled egg, or, sometimes, a slice or two of bacon. In the middle of the morning, and the middle of the afternoon, she'd walk out to where he was working, bringing a billy of tea and two or three fresh scones or rock cakes, and they'd sit together in the shade for a while.

That was when she wasn't working with him. If it was a day when they were working together she'd take something she'd made, wrapped in a cloth, and they'd drink from the water bag.

And every lunch time he came home. He'd thought that people stopped growing when they turned twenty-one, but that didn't seem to apply to him, now that he was married.

It wasn't that he grew any taller, it was in other places that he grew: his chest and arms, and legs. With his great bushy beard people laughingly called him Ned Kelly, though his hair wasn't red, and he didn't want to fight the world.

Most days he saw her walking up into the forest, and he'd stop and watch her as she walked, skirts lifted away from the dust and grass seeds. He wondered what she did there, but was too shy to ask, though he did worry a little about snakes.

For a long time he didn't notice anything.

There was always work, and, big and strong though he was, at the end of the day he was tired. Taking off his heavy boots on the verandah and cooling his feet in a basin of water outside the house left his mind in a kind of a sleep. She stood behind him, her arms over his shoulders, and they gazed over their land as the evening haze turned their world a dreamy blue.

It took a long time for him to see, this man who saw everything nature did, but when he did it hit him like the kick of a horse. He didn't know what to do. He couldn't talk to her about it, and he didn't know where to look when she was with him.

She didn't say anything, either. But she laughed a lot, and brought more flowers into the house, and made lots of special crusty bread.

Out in the paddocks he began thinking more than he'd ever thought before.

Then he stopped thinking, and began to build.

A cradle.

That cradle wasn't made—it was *built!*

Every piece of timber was special, with a special shape or a special colour, each with a different grain running like fairy paths through the forest.

He didn't hurry as he worked the timber into the right shapes, and smoothed it and polished it to bring out its warmth. He didn't really need to hurry, as he had many months before it would be needed.

All through the autumn he worked, and the winter, on days when he had an hour or two to spare. It had to be finished by spring: even he knew that. It was the same with the sheep, though he didn't say that to her.

It *was* finished by spring, the day after the last winter rains swept away to the hills leaving the wet wattle blossoms glistening like yellow sapphires.

It was finished, but it wasn't a cradle.

It was a little cathedral.

Going into town each week became a little difficult for him.

He'd help her up onto the sulky and cluck the oldening horse off down the hill to their gate. As he swung it open the horse would amble through and wait for him to shut it and climb on again, and he'd have a quick look at her.

Her back had always been straight, but now it seemed to be even straighter, as though she was trying to make herself stronger. He thought she may've been trying to make more room, inside, and he wondered at her, sitting beside him, with her hands clasped gently over her lap.

Sometimes she caught him looking at her, and she smiled at him, and he was glad that he had a beard so that she wouldn't see the redness creeping over his cheeks.

He forgot that her eyes weren't his eyes.

They only went to town on fine days—she said she didn't mind driving in the wet but he always seemed to have to do something else on rainy days: the sheep should be looked at, or he'd pull out some weeds in the new orchard because it was easier when the ground was damp, or he'd sit in front of the fire, drying off after doing something else, while she filled the room with the smell of fresh scones.

The horse seemed to know, too, picking her way around the potholes, walking slowly through the long wet patches, and even stopping to munch the green grass where purple flowers tumbled down a bank.

As they left the bush and clopped into town the difficult time began.

People came out of their weatherboards and waved from verandahs or came down to their gates and called out to them. Her, really, as he tried to look ahead and stop the horse from bolting. The horse had never bolted in its life, but you never knew, with small boys running along behind.

He'd tie up at the rail outside the store and lift her down in his strong arms, spinning his mind around them both so that they were the only people in the world, her and him...and a little bit of tomorrow.

Then she'd go inside. He'd put the nosebag on the horse, and wonder again how she could snuffle away without any oats going up her nose, or making her sneeze.

Men talked to him, about their stock, about the railway that might be built, about the rains and what a good season was coming up.

They *didn't* talk about what he was thinking most about, and he was glad. That wouldn't've been right. Not for the men, anyway.

Usually he had to get a few things in the town, for the farm, and the time went pleasantly enough.

But he always looked for her being ready, to go home.

Everyone, he was sure, wanted them to have a boy.

What *he* wanted he kept to himself, deep inside so that if it didn't happen that way nobody'd know—not even him!

The time came, as it does, and he was down in the far paddock. She'd been restless for days. That morning she'd lain in bed, tossing, her face more at the wall than towards him. She didn't smile for him.

Breakfast was a thick crust. Afraid, he forgot to close the door as he left, tying up his boots, not saying goodbye.

He went to the far paddock because. . . because. . . he had to walk. What had he done? When would it be over?

Sheep stumbled and jostled away from him. He didn't see them.

Magpies sang their happiest of spring songs. He didn't hear them.

Gentle September breezes played over his face. He didn't feel them.

All around was new life, but he was *between* life and life, waiting.

For a few more days, or perhaps a week.

A cry dreamt through the soft air, a far cry from somewhere far off. . . from. . .

From up the hill! From their house! From her!

He must get to the horse! He must fetch someone! It wasn't time yet!

Moretimemoretime—he had to have more time! But IT *WAS* TIME!

She cried again, for him.

And he was beside her, in front of her, his big and awkward hands gentling the new life as it pushed out, pushed out into his great hands.

And she slept.

For a week his boots stayed clean, soles and heels, never touching the ground.

People came and went, smiled, patted his back, brought over things. A shawl, a hand-knitted quilt, little things.

He hadn't known it before, not really, but he knew it now—he knew that he loved.

Her, and their daughter. His baby daughter.

How could it be? How could a man's heart fill and fill, and go on filling, without crushing lungs and limbs and life itself?

There was one thing, though. He was very glad that no one saw him, or heard him, striding about his paddocks, saying 'Dad...Dad. . .Dad. . .'

Long before he should've, he took the little one out with him, cradled in his arms, as though he were a great forest red gum and she a frail nest of twigs.

He propped her up against stumps while he worked, or against rocks or logs, and picked her up when she, craning to see what he was doing, forgot how not to fall over.

She chuckled and laughed, and tried hard to reach her arms all the way around his neck, her nose thrusting through his beard and pressing against his teeth.

Everything took longer to do. Before he fixed the gate he had to show her the problem, and explain why they needed so many gates on a farm, and then discuss with her how it should be mended, listening very closely to her opinions.

Quite often he hung her from a tree, in a harness he'd made out of an old bag and some strong twine. She'd swing there for hours, revolving slowly as the wind blew, loving to be taller than him, crowing, and learning the language of the bush.

Several times a day her mother'd come down to where they were, and take her, and hold her, and feed her, while he went off a little way till they'd finished.

Until then he hadn't realised that two people could be equally pleased and peaceful, the one empty, the other full.

Then came the four boys, sweeping through the farm like a tide. One son after another, new lights in his life.

Though he'd never seen the ocean, that was what it was like.

At times the tide was like locusts, and he wondered how he'd keep the food up to them.

At others it was like a hurricane, bending the wheat to the ground, and he wondered how he'd save enough for market.

Each one he took out to the paddocks, long before he should've.

Some hung in the harness while the hot winds blew the red dust around. One hung there with a sort of umbrella over him, catching the rain in his pudgy hands, already strong, and with dirt under his finger nails.

Each had his go in the harness, till he found the three of them spinning the fourth around and round, the twine tightening round his yelling, red, giddy head. But he didn't stop the unspinning, and laughed and laughed as his youngest son unwound and then tried to walk when they lifted him out.

It was good. It was what life was about, though he didn't think of it like that then.

But there was more to do. Much more. And the days didn't lengthen enough to fit it all in.

The house shrank, or so it seemed, long before the last boy arrived. Even putting some of the things in the old tent only helped for a while.

So they tramped the farm for a new site, large enough for the new house, and a vegetable garden, and a bigger chook run. He didn't like the idea of leaving the hill, but there was no room, and the soil wasn't really very good up there.

They chose a spot right down near the river. There was some flat ground a little way up a gentle slope that was just right, she said. The river flat was just right for the vegetable garden, and if they had a flood it wouldn't matter too much. The chook run would go nicely between the house and the vegetables, up the hill a bit.

She spoke as though she could see it all, as though it was already built, with smoke drifting up into the soft evening air, a wide verandah all around.

And that's the way it was, nearly two years later.

He'd always known that the years came and went, like the seasons.

That sun followed rain. That life was always there, or on the way, growing, or sleeping before growth.

That something which was the soil, the air, the forest, the land gave meaning.

But over all these had come to him something that was more. He didn't know what it was—*had*n't known what it was—until it'd gone.

They'd stood on the new platform, watching the last smudge of smoke faze into the heat, shimmering over the line that led to some far-off war in some far-off desert land, leaving them long before a daughter should have. Leaving them for . . .?

And the boys'd gone, too, to new farms, to a new paddle wheeler on the great brown river, one even to work on a newspaper in the city.

And then, suddenly, as suddenly and easily as sleep, as the sun stretched its light fingers through the morning windows, he was alone.

The magpies sang on the roof; the crows blacked across the limitless clear sky; the land warmed; insects began their dreamy summer hum.

But his soul had fled . . .

Somehow, too, the colours of life seemed to fade.

Standing on the flat ground by the river, the great forest trees at the top of the hill seemed to be greyer, their bark not quite so brown or green or red, their leaves not so lively in the evening breeze.

What does a man do when he falls alone?

He'd been alone before—but he hadn't known. He'd been building a farm. Then he'd been building a future, and he certainly wasn't alone then! Was it really over thirty years?! Nearer forty, though it seemed . . .

timeless. And it'd been so full, of building and planting
and harvesting, and driving into town . . . and growing,
and laughing, and . . .

What *does* a man do when he's alone?

He gets on with it.

Farms have to be farmed. Fences have to be mended. Fruit trees have to be pruned—but not in the
middle of summer! Make sure the dams are holding
the water; patch where needed. Fix the sails on the
top windmill, and grease the pistons on all of them.
Shoe the horse. Get some new wire netting and nails
to keep the foxes out of the chook run for a few more
years. Build a new loading pen and ramp for the
sheep—he'd been meaning to do that for a while (much
easier to drive them up a ramp than man-handle them
into the wagon).

And he has to learn to cook again, to 'keep body
and soul together' as he said to anyone who came out

to see him. There was a bit of darning to do, too, but not all that much: holes in his socks had never bothered him in the old days, why should they now? He was a man of the land.

Sometimes, not nearly often enough, there'd be a letter from one of the boys, and he'd fidget and fudge while the postman had a cup of tea and a yarn, itching for his friend to go so he could get to the crumpled lines.

Lines that led out to the mighty Murray River, to presses and ink, to a farm where it seemed to rain every day of the year. They told him about running into snags when the river was low, and having to pump for their lives (he took that with a grain of salt— they could've walked away from the boat, if the river was that low).

They told him about machines that could rumble out hundreds of newspapers an hour; of dairies with forty or fifty fat cows to milk, morning and night; of children being born, and sent off to school. He wondered if any of them swung from a tree in an old bag.

Thus does a man when he's alone, but he had to admit that it wasn't as easy as it used to be.

Four boys can be a bit of a help, and you get used to them being there; you stock the farm for five workers, you buy those extra cattle or sheep (or keep a few more than you would've if you'd been on your own). You plant more wheat.

He *had* started to wind back a little as the boys drifted off, but he'd felt good and he didn't want to see the farm go right back to the old days, before she'd come.

After a while he noticed that a few more people seemed to be coming out and dropping in for a couple of minutes, to 'see how he was doing'. Usually they'd have one of their boys with them, who'd slope off and 'look around' while cups of tea were made and drunk in the kitchen. Later he'd find that there'd been some wood cut, or a fence mended, or the chook pen cleaned out.

It made him a little cross, but he couldn't stop them.

Did they think he was getting too old to do those things for himself?!

They mightn't have, but his sons certainly did. One day they'd all turned up at the farm, without a word of warning, without their families.

He'd been delighted, though a little suspicious. Treats like that only happened at Christmas, and then only one or two of the families came at a time, the wives bringing real life back to the kitchen and the kids scattering the chooks around the yard like exploding feather pillows.

The boys were cheerful, though they looked a bit

serious, and they'd spent quite a bit of time poking around the place, looking at their old bedrooms and the firewood box, checking the sheds.

They'd brought out some cold meats from the town, and some bottles covered in ice, and in the heat of the day they'd all sat around on the veranda, talking quietly, cutting off hunks of bread, and looking over the river and valley to the hills.

He kept on looking at them, these men of his, waiting for what'd brought them. It was a long time in coming, but it came, and it came with a truth that he knew, and he was glad that it came from them, and it began with the best word of all.

'Dad. We think it's time you turned it in.'

'The farm's getting too much for you.'

'You're not as young as you used to be, you know.'

'We don't like you being so far away from everybody.'

Each of them'd said something. He couldn't re-member *what* they'd said, now, but he could still hear what it *sounded like*, and how they'd looked when they said it.

Some of the colours came back as he listened, though what they were saying meant so much. They couldn't know *how* much.

They were asking him to leave his farm.

He did.

But not to the thriving dairy farm the two youngest owned, down in the soft and misty hills of the south.

Nor down to the great Murray River which lifted the paddle steamers forty feet to the high wharf at E-chuca when the river was up.

And certainly not to the city, even though they printed a newspaper every day of the week, morning and night, except Sundays.

He shifted into town.

Some old friends had done the same thing a few years before, and they offered him a cheery room at the back of the house they'd settled in.

Living in town was different. He could talk to people almost whenever he wanted to, people he'd known for years but had never really had a good long chat with.

Something always seemed to be happening: the train came in twice a week, and left twice a week, the next morning; at least once a month someone got married in the little church he'd helped build; and for various reasons that he never quite understood there'd be two or three nights each year when everybody let off firecrackers and rockets.

They were very good to him, his old friends—she cooked him lovely meals and did his washing and things, and they'd spend most evenings in the front room, playing cards or listening to the radio, or just talking in front of the fire.

He was never short of company.

And he never really had anything to do.

Then the letter came!

Dear Dad,

The newspaper's gone bust.

Can I come home and take over the farm?

He suddenly discovered that living in the town wasn't so bad after all: the house was next to the Post Office and the Post Office was open and he was in there writing the telegram before the postie'd blown his whistle next door!

Yes! Dad.

Though they wouldn't let him put in the exclamation mark. And they charged him for twelve words.

And he hardly sat still for the next ten days, waiting for the train to steam his oldest son home.

Together they squeezed into the seat of his old friend's ute, their bags thrown in the back, and they laughed as they drove out the rutted track to the farm.

But he didn't move into the house down by the river. He knew that one day a girl with the dry land in her eyes would smile at his son, and that *they* should have the house for themselves.

He climbed the hill to his first house, and the few shreds of tent which hung like faded but not-altogether-defeated pennants from the broken ridge pole.

It took him quite a long time to get up there, and he was puffing a bit when he arrived, but he didn't mind. Only a few days were needed to get things cleaned up, and his son gave him a hand, in between working on the river house.

Once again he sat out the front, looking over his farm, his *son*'s farm, to the far hills.

Slowly contentment began to creep back.

Up here he was next to the forest, and he began doing what he used to see *her* doing most days.

Although it was faint almost to illusion he knew the path she used to take, around the back, past the water tank and the remains of their first chook house, and over the fence on the style he'd built the first week she'd come.

He'd always gone into the forest further down, at the gate, because that was what gates were for and he always had some wood to lug back. He hadn't realised that it was far better to go into the forest by *her* way, and he started to joke to himself about 'going in style'.

Now that he didn't have to look for timber to cut he had time to look at the forest, and he began to see why she'd gone into it so often.

It was a world where the trees shaped each other, opening up to let the sun fall on glades of wallaby grass or nodding pygmy orchids or bronze-scaled lizards sleeping alertly on warm rocks.

As it had with her, the forest took him in as he walked slowly along its paths. It shaded him and warmed him, breathed into him and lulled him, and called him.

Slowly he forgot the farm. Less and less did he look out over the river to the hills. Now he looked *away* from his land, into his forest, which she had found before him.

His forest, which had given him his house and his children's cradle, and their dresser and cupboards and table and chest.

And he realised that it'd been *his* forest all along, even back when he'd built his first fence and frightened the wild animals with his axe blows and hearty singing.

He stood and looked at his forest, this tree of an old man amongst older giants, his back to the rough bark.

And the bark roughed his skin caressingly as he slipped slowly down against the trunk to the ground.

And there he went—a man finally alone, with his trees and his birds, his wind, his rain.

His *her*...

And his son, striding up the hill towards the old house, fresh eggs in a billy.

And news in his eyes.

What Do I Have To Do?

The old brass doorbell rang, not as loudly as usual.

An old man came into the shop, walking quite slowly, as if he wasn't too sure about things.

'G'day,' I said. 'Can I help you?'

He looked around as the floor creaked beneath his sandals.

'A lovely day,' I said. 'Very warm for this time of year.'

There was something familiar about him, though I was sure that he wasn't a local.

'Down for the day?' I asked. 'It's nice on the beach when the wind's off-shore.'

Reaching the counter he rested a wrinkled hand beside the big lolly jar.

'People come here from all over. The cliffs are said to be the finest in Australia.'

He gave a little smile. I thought he was going to say something then, but he didn't.

'It's fairly quiet at present. Good for you—you don't have to hang around all day to get served.'

I didn't think that he'd mind too much, if he'd had to wait. Time seemed less important with him in the shop. It didn't worry me that he wasn't the chatty type—you get sick of people who can't stop talking. Still, I *was* in business and I'd never sell him anything if he didn't say something.

'What would you like? We've got just about everything here.'

His crinkled eyes looked at the shelves and he gave a bit of a shrug.

'I can't see any jelly babies.'

His voice seemed to come from everywhere, deep, like waves echoing in a great cave.

'No,' I laughed. 'You've hit on the one thing I'm out of! What about fruit pastilles? Black currant ones. They're my favourite.'

I waited, eagerly, for him to speak.

'Fruit pastilles?' His voice sounded better than my favourite lollies, even though he spoke a little uncertainly.

'I strongly recommend them. My wife makes them, fresh every summer. They're the best in the world.'

'In the world? Nobody makes better ones?'

I shook my head, popping one of the pastilles into my mouth. My eyes closed as the delicious sweet started to melt, spreading the tangy taste around my tongue. 'They're absolutely heavenly.'

He gave a little start.

'We call them Paradise Pastilles,' I said blissfully.

He looked at me keenly. 'I really wanted jelly babies,' he said, 'but if you say they're that good I'll have some.'

I measured a good quantity into a white paper bag and gave them to him.

'Have them. They're on me,' I said. I didn't usually give things away, especially my wife's pastilles.

'Thank you very much indeed,' he said.

I felt good: really good. 'You're not from around here?'

He was popping a pastille into his mouth, though it looked strangely like a jelly baby.

'Well, yes and no,' he said, slightly apologetically.

'Oh,' I said. 'Yes. I didn't think you were a local. But you *do* seem a little familiar to me.'

'Do I?! Most people don't seem to know me.'

His face became a little sad, in a puzzled kind of way.

I tried to cheer him up. 'Don't worry about that. Only pop stars and royalty are really well known. And even that doesn't last for very long with most of them. Especially pop stars.'

'I've been around for quite a long time,' he said. 'I thought people would know me, and come up and say hello and everything.'

'People have pretty short memories,' I said. 'Were you in the movies?'

'You really don't know me?' he said.

'Well, no, not really. Although....'

'What about my....?'

'Your beard? Yes, there's something about that, I must admit.'

'And my....?'

'Your walking stick? No, lots of people have those. Older people.'

'It's not a walking stick. It's a staff.'

'Oh. I see. Yes, well...'

'And what about this?'

'Er...I'm not too sure,' I said. The light was shining from behind him, making it a bit difficult to see what he was pointing at.

'It's a halo,' he said.

'A halo?!'

'A halo.'

'A halo!? But they're only worn by....!'

'By angels.'

'By ANGELS! But you don't look like an angel!'

'Not even the Archangel Gabriel?'

'Well, yes, perhaps....But you're not him...are you?'

'No.'

'Oh. I thought not.'

'Angels aren't the only ones who wear haloes, you know.'

'Yes, well, um, ah, er, well...of course not....they're also worn by...good God....you're not....!'

He looked a little pleased at my amazement.

'With a capital G,' he said.

The pastille *had* turned into a jelly baby!

'Um...ah...er...well...yes...I can see why you're a little upset that people don't know you. Of course, I had a bit of an idea. It was just that I...ah...wasn't expecting you. I mean, it's not every day that...'

'Usually you can't see me.'

My face grew very red.

'Don't worry,' he said. 'Everybody does things they're ashamed of.'

'Even you?!' I cried, with relief that he wasn't going to tell my wife.

He gave a cough. 'I meant every human.'

'Yes, of course,' I agreed quickly. I was afraid that he might change his mind, about talking to my wife. 'I'm sorry about the jelly babies.'

'That's all right. It doesn't really make much difference to me.'

'No. I can see that now.'

I didn't quite know what to say next. What *do* you say next, in that situation? He still looked kind of sad, and puzzled, not at all as he should've looked, except for the wonderful beard, and the staff, and the shimmering halo.

'Is there something I can help you with?' I said, not very hopefully. After all, I was only a shopkeeper.

He turned and looked at me, and I felt that I'd never been properly looked at before.

'There might be,' he said. 'What do I have to do?'

I looked at him blankly, which wasn't very intelligent, I know, but I couldn't think of any other way to look when he said that.

'What do I have to *do*?'

'What do you have to do for what?' I asked.

'What do I have to do to make people come up to me, and talk to me, and hold my hand, and do all those sorts of things?'

I could see what he meant. You *would* be a bit careful, if you knew who he was, wouldn't you?

`It's been such a long time since anyone's touched me. You know, in a *lov*ing sort of way.'

`Oh, dear. That *is* bad! That's awful! We must do something about *that*!'

`Can we?! Do you know what I can do? Oh, I'm so pleased that I came into your shop!'

I began to think. I thought and thought. I wasn't all that good at thinking, but I *had to be* this time.

`I have it!' I cried. `That's it!'

'You know what I have to do?!' he almost shouted, shaking the jars on the shelves and turning all my wife's fruit pastilles into jelly babies.

I reached up to his ear—I hadn't realised how tall he was before—and whispered.

A great smile bloomed across his face and I knew I'd live forever.

`You're right! You're absolutely right! I'll do it!!'

I'm not at all sure what happened next. As he went out of the shop there might've been a puff of smoke, or a flash of lightning, or both. Whatever happened, suddenly the empty street turned into hundreds of people, cheering and smiling and laughing and reaching out, pressing in close to the door of my shop.

And, as I looked, *Princess Diana* turned towards me.

And winked.

Her tiara, shimmering happily in her hair, looking strangely like a halo.

The Japs

*[WW2 Japanese interred thousands of allied
soldiers after Singapore capitulated, 15th
February 1942]*

Shouting. Explosions. *Banzai! Banzai!*
Crashing. Shouting. Screaming. *The Japs!
Japs! Look out! Get out!* Screaming. Shouting.
Shooting. Explosions.

Boots running down the main passage. Clumping
up the stairs, the fire escape. She rushed to the theatre
door, yelling for the others to help. Screams. Shots.
Upstairs, everywhere. Slammed it shut, dragged desks
over, filing cabinets, operating equipment, jammed
against door, pushing desperate weight against it.

Door shuddering, juddering, splitting, cracking, desks toppling, screaming Japanese erupting over them, a tsunami of terror.

She wondered, fleetingly, as she was hurled to the floor, glimpsing Parkinson's body falling beside her, his neck slashed by a dirty bayonet, whether there would be a time with Twiggy, when this was all over. Clothes ripped off, violently. One after another they entered her, rolling her over, this way and that way, one after another, a war within a war, one after another, again and again, another, another; shouting, thrusting, mouths frothing; the last penetration, the final violent penetration, the *un-felt* penetration of a sixteen-inch Japanese bayonet.

The gentle lapping of the warm salty oily harbour waters, gentling her broken body under the flickering light of sinking ships...

It wasn't too bad at first, once internment was accepted. Selarang Barracks became a sort of home, an hour or so's drive out at Changi. The Japs initially pretty well left them all to their own devices, but without weapons.

Some of them who'd been Home before the war referred to the place laughingly as Butlin's, but this wore thin very quickly, changing to sardonic, ironic, and loathing.

Defeat had to be quickly changed to manageable imprisonment, to order and engagement.

Order came with reconstituting, as far as possible, the dispersed and disjointed tens of thousands of men into their previous units.

Engagement was a more difficult matter.

Food turned out to be an unexpected solution. Their captors gave them none for the first two weeks—meals were what was left of their rations, or that could be scrounged. Then began the rice regime—every meal, occasionally with a hint of meat, and increasingly bitter complaints about the food "giving us the shits". Ironic, because it actually did the opposite.

They needn't have worried, though, because the runs came soon enough, in Bradmanesque quantities.

Someone decided to give a lecture on something—it might have been Willbourn on geology—and quite soon Changi University was under way, but music and comedy soon proved to be the most popular activity, with the Southern Area Concert Party and Bill Middleton and his orchestra, and female impersonators like Bobby Spong, magnificently reminding everyone why the war was being fought.

In this vein, the Malay Volunteer Force decided that a Gilbert & Sullivan opera should be their contribution—lots of opportunities for inappropriate lyrics—and that, in the circumstances, they couldn't go past *The Mikado*.

♪*If you want to know who we are, We are gentlemen of*

Japan♪.

"Twiggy", the battalion Padre, of course, would be Lord High Executioner, because of his impressive height and because no-one thought that he could possibly execute anyone. Maybe bore them to death with one of his tropical sermons! Its first, and only, performance was, naturally, on April 29th –the Emperor's Birthday–to a riotously delighted audience, with universal acclamation. Universal acclamation, that is, apart from a very small number of victorious dissidents who arranged thirty days' solitary confine-ment on starvation rations for the entire cast and orchestra and production team and the first two rows of the audience.

As well as listing them in U Party to be sent to build a railway.

Reports began to drift in, like a poisoned mist, of massacres of Chinese, of countless bayonettings, drownings, shootings, hangings, decapitations—the *kapara potong*[1] had transferred from Nanking to Singapore—and of a Nip—who could believe this?!—issuing safe conduct passes to thousands of Chinese and others who (he believed) would not then take up arms again against the Japanese.

What is it about us that we can do such things, at the same time, in the same place?

Does—can—good *ever* ease the horrors of bad?

Cynthia left the house in Cairnhill Road, picking her way carefully around craters and rubble and clouds of flies, intending to go to the hospital to see whether she could help in some way.

---

[1] Beheadings.

It was so eerie, after the capitulation. *We ruled an Empire!* What now? Her mind was a blank. *They must do something about the bodies.* It was not far from the sea, but far enough that no breeze reached the hospital's white, shrapnel-pitted walls. She went up the front steps, through the great, shattered front door. The passage was littered with papers and clothes, all smeared with darkening blood, her thin plimsolls sticking tardily to the floor as she moved further into the passage. Not thinking, she found herself in the second floor operating theatre. It felt of death, not unforeseen, unwanted death but death by violent design, merciless, quick, violent. Death echoed from the red-streaked walls, from the broken light shades, from the door handles. Air! She opened the window, looked down at sparse green-ery, the sea a little way. *Oh, God! How...!?*

A slight noise behind.

'Mac!' Her whole body shivered as it remembered what had so nearly happened at **Punggol Beach**, that she had wanted so much to happen.

'Cynthia?'

'What...what are you doing...here?'

'Scrounging. We need things. The Japs seem to have other things on their minds.'

The light was behind her, but memory of her was suddenly throughout his mind.

'Please...hold me.' A voice of fright, of need.

He held her, quivering, stroking her hair, calming the sobs.

The shuddering lessened, stopped. She looked up at him, a wan smile thanking him.

'You didn't get away.'

'I felt I had to stay. It didn't seem quite...right. What will happen to us, Mac?'

Everything, or nothing! 'I don't know.'

'Do you remember Punggol, Mac? That night?'

It was a night that he'd regretted ever since, when courage had deserted him, when he was totally uncertain about what she wanted.

She slowly turned in his arms, drawing them down, around her waist, drawing his hand down into her shorts, slowly moving her body forwards and back into his. She felt his strength and desire, and forgot the pre-war beach, turning to capture his mouth and pull him onto the operating table.

Future or no future, it was the last time for them both.

They were going to build a railway that couldn't be built. Later, much later, those that returned told stories about others, never about themselves. That is how we know.

They crossed into Siam at Padang Besar, where Mac thought briefly about the Thais that bind, then thought erratically about why he'd thought such a silly thought.

Six months of poor quality rice and a teaspoon of meat twice a week, and whatever could be scrounged, had ill-prepared the six hundred men for the four day journey, cramped cheek-by-jowl in steel railway trucks, slowly roasting, to Bam Pong. Nor for the three-week, hundred-mile march through the soaking monsoon, to Kinsaiyok and Hellfire Pass.

Twiggy looked up at the jungle-strewn hills, but there didn't appear to be much aid coming from that direction. *"For I know the plans I have for you,"* declares the Lord, *"plans to prosper you and not to harm you, plans to give you hope and a future."*

Was it different back then, those thousands of years ago, when David wrote those words? Did God actually come to *his* aid, or was it like today, as with all other days (it seemed), that He was otherwise engaged?

He jerked the sweat from his brows—not that it made any difference—hoping that none of his fellows stolidly marching in front of him, behind him, had seen these thoughts.

But thinking can't be stopped so easily, thoughts don't dissipate as easily as sweat from an exhausted brow—they so easily flow into new pathways, or the same pathways, or uncomfortable pathways. *Why doesn't He respond to my prayers?* This had been bothering him for some time; actually since he'd seen those heads impaled on rough stakes, near the station in Singapore. *Why is there Evil?* This was a big one. He thought of Covent Garden and the market stalls stretching into the distance under the arched roof as Mummy sought out the best fruit, taking this apple, rejecting that, taking this strawberry, rejecting that—sorting the good from the bad. *Is that what I've been doing? Sorting the good into the God basket and the bad into the...? But if God created every thing He must have created everything...*

Even belly buttons! *But Adam couldn't have had a belly button, nor Eve. And why didn't He just create Eve, as He did with Adam? Why make her from one of Adam's ribs? Why did He give Adam a spare rib in the first place? ...We speak of the wisdom of God, hidden in a mystery...*

Up Country—that is what many of them thought, but if they did, no-one could have said why they called it this. For all anyone knew they might have been in an underwater cavern, drowning, strangling in a hopeless, tangled mess of vile seaweed vines.

Mac looked around, his aching frame struggling to achieve a more-or-less perpendicular state. Adapt or perish. Adapt or *evolve?* Were these people, his friends, human? Are we becoming a *new species?* Are we some new species born of unknown jungle tangle-weeds? The yellow men were certainly human, no bones about it. *They* were human, *we* are not. Proper humans, fair dinkum soldiers, as the Aussies would say, don't get captured; don't give up; fight to the death; serve their Emperor; die for their Emperor. Honour. *We* slave for *their* Emperor, *we* die for *their* Emperor. What does *our* Emperor do?

Another day, another day carrying sick comrades on backs, another day forced to go to the bridge and haul and place logs, even if it had to be done in a sitting position.

Malaria, dengue, hookworm. beriberi, gastroenteritis, tropical ulcers, scabies, ringworm, boils, diphtheria, cholera, dysentery–Twiggy had had them all–he was a compendium of tropical diseases, a walking hospital ward.

Had been for weeks. For *ever*, it seemed. Except for the walking. He would have laughed. *Walking!*

When had he ever *walked*!

He didn't want to go, it was too far to the latrines, too far to the steps from his so-called bed, and there couldn't be anything left in him to make a deposit, anyway.

But the pain was excruciating.

♪*When other helpers fail and comforts flee, Help of the helpless, O abide with me.* ♪

Abide with me! Abide with *any*one here! We're *all* helpless!

His bones and bits of hanging parchment re-arrang-ed themselves as his terminally wasted body lost its way, then found it again as it crashed onto the muddy floor. The attap roof might as well have been in London. Erratic lightning showed the way, would have shown the way, if he'd been interested. London! The merest thought, meaningless, like the week-long journey to the lats. A wraith, he jagged painfully down the steps, not conscious of the pain anymore. When did hurt hurt? Meaningless. Into the mud, instinct the direction, a deep recess in his brain smiling historically at the possibility of a pun, the stink oozing all the way back here to the hospital, like a tide of demonic fire ants. Was the rain wetter, or the mud? Was he crawling or swimming? A sheet of lightning–his skeletal destination outlined against the forest; the thunder reminded him of the futile reason for continuing the struggle. No, the thunder was *inside* him, screwing him around, thrusting his nose into the mud, dragging his head up, pushing his dis-jointed joints forward, forward, forward...Sucking in the air; stinking, but air. He reached up, claws pincering the edge of the hole, fixing, hauling up, gasping into the hole, the blackness. Panting, panting, the hurt hurting, hurting, the need urgent. A final lurch upwards, onto the platform, and the cut-out hole, somehow positioning his pitiful arse for the possible squirt into the blackness, the squirt that wouldn't come, wouldn't come but the blackness did, as he started to slide, downwards, backside first, then the legs, folding upwards like a closing umbrella, then the narrow body and the arms, down, down into the deep blackness.

♪*Time, like an ever-rolling stream, soon bears us all away;*

we fly forgotten, as a dream dies at the opening day. ♪

'For Christ's sake, Twiggy, He said *beside* quiet waters, not *in* them!'

Then, like an infinity of mothers, with no baby bath but the warm water of the monsoon leeching the electricity from the firmament, Mac began to cleanse the sad, gallant English gentleman, gently stroking the filth back into the redempting soil.

Then bones, many bones, grasped him, here and there, here and there, and lifted him, and bore him and carried him softly back to the "hospital", and the monsoon wept on them, on them all, all up and down the line.

A duck egg found its way, from what mysterious, miraculous source, into his mouth.

♪*All things living God does feed; with full measure, meets their need: for God's mercies shall endure, ever faithful, ever sure.* ♪

A duck egg! Not a miracle, just many men pooling their wages—a few cents a day—negotiating with Thai sampanning traders, making the most of this unexpected silver lining in their lives.

Duck eggs, and unknown vegetables, and fruits, and strength.

Suddenly it was August 1945, August the 16th, and the biggest man-made bang in history, and a Jap guard reaching down to wreak a final vengeance on this wasted, worthless piece of shit, snarling obscenities at him, mad-driven that his God Emperor had surrendered to these worthless creatures.

Twiggy leapt up at the Jap, grabbing an unseen plank in the mud. Whack! *Bastard! Fucking bastard!* Whack! Dodging a kick! A sharp pain in the eye. Whack whack whack! *Bastards! Fucking bastards! Thompson! Robertson.* Whack. Power coursing through his recovering body. WHACK. *Paterson. Doc Stephenson.* Whack. No movement. Keep hitting.

Crack. ♪*I am the Lord... High...Executioner*♪... Whack.

Snashall. Boden. Smash. *Robinson.* SMASH. Knees bending. Strength going. Falling. Collapsing onto, into, the jelly of blood that was the remains of the hated Greater East Asia Co-Prosperity Sphere.

Rita...where...?

His war over.

Never, never, never again to speak of God's Love.

Never. Never. Never.

Ever.

Jesus would have wept.

Not Only Black

Long, long ago, even before once upon a time, there was Nothing. Nothing could be seen, nothing could be heard, and there was no-one to see or hear.

Then, one day, or it may have been one night, or it could of been some other time, the Great Nothing saw, or didn't see, Black, and it was good. But, still, Nothing could be seen. Black was not enough by itself.

So the Great Nothing caused White to appear, blinding, hot, hot; yet there was no-one to be blinded or burnt.

And White was not Black, and Black was not White, and the Great Nothing caused them to be in Balance, one after the other and one before the other, and there was Change.

And that was the First Day.

Time passed, White followed Black, Black followed White, neither being seen, neither could be seen.

But when there was Black there was no White, and when there was White there was no Black: the Great Nothing saw that Balance was not enough.

So the Great Nothing took little bits of White and sprinkled them over Black. And little bits of Black and floated them through White. And so was created Contrast.

And that was the Second Day.

Though Contrast was pleasing, Black was still Black, and White was still White.

One came, then went; the other came, then went. All was sharp and edged.

All was sudden. All was same. All was even.

There was too much Balance.

And so the Great Nothing mixed some Black with some White and caused Grey, and placed it between Black and White, White and Black, and there was created Shade.

And that was the Third Day.

There was Balance and Contrast, Change and Shade, Black and White and Grey.

The greatest of these was Change, but the Great Nothing saw that even this was not enough, even though Black changed to White through Grey, and White changed to Black through Grey, and White followed Grey and Black followed Grey, and Grey followed Black and Grey followed White, and Black had some White and White had some Black.

There must be more Contrast.

And so the Great Nothing created Red and Blue and Yellow.

There was Colour, and Contrast: much Contrast.

And that was the Fourth Day.

Black and White. Black and Grey. White and Grey. Black and White and Grey.

Black and Red. Black and Blue. Black and Yellow. White and Red. White and Blue. White and Yellow. Grey and Red. Grey and Blue. Grey and Yellow.

Colour.

Contrast.

Change. Some, but not much.

So the Great Nothing allowed all that was created to mix together, in pleasing ways.

And so there became Tones.

And that was the Fifth Day.

Blue and Red. Red and Yellow. Yellow and Blue. Blue and Red and White. Red and Yellow and White. Blue and Yellow and White. Red and Blue and Yellow and White. Azure and Lavender and Coral and Ochre and Gold and Cobalt and Turquoise and Cornflower and Magenta and Violet and many, many others.

But all this beauty, unorganised and chaotic, began running together, mingling, darking, to make Near-Black.

Like Nothing.

So the Great Nothing made rain, and Light through the rain, and created Rainbow.

And that was the Sixth Day.

And on the seventh day the Great Nothing did nothing, and he's done nothing ever since!

Uncle Gareth's Potted
History of Himself

Yes, Amber, sweetheart, it was long ago. We
had a Black and White, but not Colour. It
was before you was born, though probably
more'n a cuppla fellas'd tried to sneak ya in before the
actual event! But that would've been with different
mothers so you shouldn't worry about that too much.
You might have been a boy. Or a diff'rent colour.
Anyways, the Korean War was well'n truly behind us—
what's that?—that was when we was all up there savin'
the bastards who'd guarded us to death on the Railway,
savin' the Koreans from the Koreans and the Koreans
from the Chinese—what's that?—yair the Chinese'd been
on our side but somehow they'd changed colour and
we had to stop 'em, or at least that's what the Yanks

said we hadta do, if we didn't mind a little inconvenience, so off we went agen. Funny thing was that we didn't stop at Singapore on the way up from Auckland that time which a few of us thought was a bloody good thing, if you'll pardon my French. Yair, *they* had a lot to answer for, later, which they never did—what's that?—the bloody French, if you'll pard'n my...well, you know... anyways, we had to go up there agen, Vietnam this time, with the Aussies, 'coz the Yanks said we hadta 'coz if we didn't then the dominos'd get us, which I didn't understand, Monopoly bein' me game an' all that. We was surprised we didn't get off at Singapore 'coz the Chinese was shootin' everyone up in Malaya, yair that was before Lee Kuan Yew took over Singapore. Yair he was Chinese but not the Chinese kind of Chinese, if ya know what I mean. Big fish inna small pond; tried a bigger pond once but didn't like it. Once they get ya on a boat that's it, ya can end up anywhere and usually did. The trick was ta come back! Which not everybody did and some of those that did didn't really, if ya know what I mean. Yer Dad might have been one of those but probably not; never could tell in those days. Not even nowadays when they say one thing before they get elected 'n' do the other when they git in. Not that they're diffrent from the old days just diffrent buggers. Anyways, as I was sayin', after Black and White and before Colour, maybe when Landy stopped racin' ta pick up Ron Clarke. Yair, that was a Noble thing; doesn't happen nowadays; someone falls over—could be here in the Delights—and all ya do is call the amblicance and go home for ya dinner. Outa a packet outa the fridge! What's wrong with a Coolgardie Safe?! A bitta punctured metal, a bitta canvas, a bitta water and Bob's ya Uncle the butter's hard as a rock! Then ol' Uncle Bob come back, with his bushy eyebrows and plummy accent and Lord of the Sinkin' Bloody Pommy Bastards' Ports![2] Stone the flamin' crows!

---

[2] Warden of the Cinque Ports, I think. *Ed.*

Next thing they'll be knight'n the bloody Queen,
pard'n me French. Nah, Colour's the thing. Useta go
round to me mate's father-in-law's and look in the
windah 'coz you couldn't have a tele in the tent. Stone
the crows! ya shoulda seen the kafuffle when me mate
discov-ered all that nickel out at Mt Windarra—the
fancy boys at the stock exchanges musta wet
theirselves! They was pushin' an' shovin' an' yellin' an'
screamin' an' wettin' theirselves and we was up there
sittin' on the stuff, laughin' our heads off. Woulda
been better buyin' some shares! But kay serrah serrah,
as Doris Day always said, what doesn't getcha makes
ya stronga. I shoulda joined the circus by now! *Teddy
Bear*, the world's strongest man outa Changi etc etc, by
Royal Bloody Appointment! Life's a circus, ain't it, a
three-bloody-ring circus with Bob bloody Menzies the
lord of the rings and his mates till Gough the Great
knocked 'em all off! Ah, them was the days, pity they
was only weeks, really. Luna Park, it was, Canberra,
Lunatic Park, same as always, dunno why we vote for

them, though I don't—gets closetrophobic in them
polling booths or whatever they're called. Shoulda
made *The Don* Prime Minister, or Ritchie, or Bobby, or
Tubby, or even Dicky Bird but he was a Pom, which
you certainly aren't, I think, but ya never knows, nowadays, with all this sharin' of mums and dads and mums
and no dads and dads and grandmothers an' so on an'
so forth an' all that. Told all me mates when you was
born, musta bored them coz they said I was talkin' like
I was ya father so I told 'em to stick it up their collec-
tive or individual arses—their choice—and use the *Questa
Casta* in future, they wouldn't be welcome at the
Delights. Yair, Amber, mates're one thing, Ambers
another. Anyways, as I might've said, it was a long
time ago.

The Old Jail

The hot tap of drought had again poured dryness over the land. This was forever nothing new, though she was too young to know that. She looked past and above her grandmother's red-streaked raven hair at the white hairy clouds, almost lost, drifting in the baking blue sky.

Will they like me?

'C'mon, Merry, let's go. No good dreamin' and sulkin' out here.'

I never dream! I don't ever sulk!

She swung her little white handbag–the one she

kept her small treasures in—behind her back. *They never look there.*

Five year-old girls don't interest screws, not even their handbags, particularly when there's a crumpled old strum-pet with red paint dripping through her dyed-black hair that they can snigger superiously at. Just another one from the scrub.

'C'm*on*!' and she was pushed once again through the thickly serious door of the old prison, like a reluctant ghost jig-jagging through a wall.

She'd been coming here forever. Waiting for the door to open. The door in the door. The small door that was still big. That had a kind of step that she had to step over. Though this seemed to be getting easier to do. Another month, another visit. Into the court-yard, the clouds suddenly framed in the past, held up there by the high, imprisoning walls.

Doors. Doors on the way in. Doors on the way out.

Doors on the houses on the streets on the long walk to these doors. She didn't know anything about what was behind those doors, only what was behind these doors. Through these doors. Visit after visit. How many doors? She didn't know. She couldn't count. How many visits? She didn't know. She couldn't count.

'Come on.' Not so gruffly, a hot, dry, wrinkled hand reaching for hers. A hand from a hot, dry, wrinkled country. *Country*. Even now she knew that it was **Country**, not **country**, or *the Bush*, or *the Outback*, or *Back of Burke*. *Her* Country. Though she was starting to know that she was just a little bit different from most of the others, her friends. And, although she'd never been there, she was quite sure that she was different from the people behind the doors.

The usual screw banged the door shut, locked it, padded after them down the path. *She smells.* The next door was just a door, the usual kind of door, the ones that always shut after her, out here. It shut behind her. The dry hand tugged her into the *Talking Room.*

Across the room another door opened. She'd never been through that door, but it always opened after they'd come into the room, and it always closed before they'd left, memories going, memories staying. Memories building on memories, more and more rememberings, more and more can't forgettings.

The Talking Room, but she didn't talk. She listened. Or...

...she *might* have been listening. Nobody looking at her could really tell. Not that anyone tried very hard, or really cared.

Across the room the door opened. The *Screwdriver* opened it. He looked into The Talking Room, and back over his shoulder. A man in a women's prison. *The* man in the women's prison. But not a black fella.

She knew that that was his name, and she knew that that wasn't his real name, like hers was Meredith. But she didn't know *why* that was his name.

It was many years before she understood the concept of irony.

Or that a name can mean many things.

'Get a move on, Kitty. They'll be gone before you've got your arse into gear.'

He pushed the woman into the room and went back to filling the doorway, knowing that that particular piece of anatomy wasn't exactly a closed door to him.

Merry moved closer to her grandmother.

'G'day, kid. Got nuthin' to say? Why'd ya bring 'er, Mum?' The woman suddenly lunged at Merry, slapping her, swinging her around.

Merry cried, struggled. *The Screwdriver* grabbed Kitty from behind, big flat hands deliberately careless in the restraining that had to be done; thrust her down onto a chair; told Merry to stop snivelling; didn't know that Merry's handbag was now a little lighter and Kitty's pocket a little heavier; didn't know, or did know. One girl's treasure another girl's pleasure.

And a man's. 'That's enough,' he snarled, without rancour, his hands cooling as the fitful airconditioning licked over them. 'Youse're out if that happens agen.'

Nothing had happened, as far as everyone else in the room was concerned. Screws were screws, kids were kids, shit happens (as they say in the classics). There was a kind of ritual in the Talking Room, a heated ritual with no heat, no energy; a ritual ritual. A ritual with hardly any point. No point, really, except to be there.

The three generations faced each other, again, the older two, seated, staring momentarily into each other's eyes, again; seeing everything, and nothing. Again. Country. It called. It filled...everything. The sun. The unseen, unseeable breezes. The creeks that were once wet, and might be again. The gums that were once young, and wouldn't be again...until the fire returned. The yams, hidden, and the digging sticks that would uncover them, amidst the chatter, and feed them all when the men finally came back to camp, empty handed. The seasons, that white fellas didn't understand but that were painted...everywhere. The way signs that white fellas didn't see but were written... everywhere.

Country. Home. Without doors.

Merry fidgeted. She was tired; she'd walked a long way. She didn't know that, really, she'd walked no-where. That was to come. In another life. She listen-ed to a magpie out there somewhere. She didn't call it "warbling", and she didn't imagine that it was singing, though she didn't know all that much about singing. She loved their black and white colours, and how they could suddenly disappear in a step or two, shadowless. *I wish I could do that.*

She wished she could go; she'd done her bit. But she had to wait. Why?

'Better be off, Kit.' *At last.*

'Yair. OK.'

'Brought ya a treat.'

Handed over a brown paper bag of heat-melting vanilla slices.

'See ya next month.'

'Yair.'

'C'mon, pet.' But Merry was already at the door, waiting for the screw to let them out. Glancing back she saw him hurrying her mother through the other door, but she couldn't see his hands.

Doors open, doors close. Sometimes—rarely?—doors closing means doors opening. The last door closed behind her and her mother, and the door that she loved opened in front—and all around her—and inside her.

The sun. The unseen, unseeable breezes. The creeks that were once wet, and would be again. The old gums, waiting for the fires to create their children, to take their places when the time came. The yams and witchetty grubs, hidden until happy chatter led to their discovery and a change of life. The painted seasons, dreaming water colours. Tracks in the bush, signposts written everywhere, if you have eyes.

Home. No doors. Country.

A Shaggy Frog Story

*Read this aloud, with feeling, as if you
were Hungarian, because you will be
revealing information hitherto unknown.
If you are already Hungarian, Slovak
will do.*

A ll is not as it zeems, Amber, in ziss strange world of ours. Ze Earth is still—it doesn't move, yes? If it moved, we would fall off it! Ze *zun* moves. Ze *moon* moves. Even ze *stars* move—you can see zis yourself when you lie on your back on ze sand all night out in ze desert. But you must stay awake!

Ah, yes, ze Earth does not move. Ziss is why Earth *things* can move! Ze wind, ze rain, ze clouds, ze branches in ze trees and zair leaves in ze trillions, and ze birds and ze bees of course and all ze uzzer living zings.

It was ze zame for Pobble. He discovered himself ze first time in ze middle of a floating field of scum thicker than ze effluents from a parliamentary dining room. Yet he did not know ziss because he was just a teensy weensy speck at ze time, in ze slime. It was ze same for you, Amber, once, but ze effluents was not so much scummified.

Lucky for Pobble, he was not in parliamentary dining room effluents. He was in frogs porn. That is like jelly, but it is wise to not eat ziss jelly, even if you have loshings of icecream. Unless you are a ducks or ze fish or ze flying insects, or any uzzer creatures zat like to eat ze frogs jellies. No, Amber, zat is not ze zame as goulash.

Zen one day, or maybe one night–nobody knows for sure–ze speck zat was to be Pobble became an egg. Ziss is not a bacon-and-egg egg but ze frog's egg.

Zere is no egg shell. If you are silly enough to zink zat frogs' eggs have shells ze yolk, as zey say, is definitely on you! Ha ha.

Anyways, ze egg zat was to be Pobble biggered and biggered, but not too much biggered or it would have frightened all ze world's posteriors to be opened in an End of Days to end all days!

No, ze egg became ze tadpole. Ziss is baby Pobble.

He grows zum legs. He loves ze water.

He also loves his brothers and sisters, which he eats.

Ziss, he says to himself, is good, and bad. Good because zey was scrumpy, bad because he was still hungry.

Zo, he finished eating his tail and climbed onto ze floating lily leaf.

"All is not as it zeemed," he zed to himself. He blinked. He had never blinked before—zat is why he zed zat all is not as it zeemed, Amber, because he had never blinked before, because tadpoles do not have eyeflaps under ze water coz zay would only keep on shutting, and not opening coz ze water pressure, you understand, Amber, would be too much for ze eye-flaps muscles to cope with, if zay had any.

Far, far away, *Quercus suber* was having his 300th birthday. Yes, Amber, zat is his proper name. Ze warmth from ze sun and ze cheekinessy breeze told him zat it was nine years, exactly, since ze day of his last barking. No, Amber, he was not a dog! He was ze cork tree; ze *old* cork tree.

Ze men came with zair axes and stuff and cut round and up and down and prised and pulled off his bark and sent it off to factory to be corks. And one of zese fell out of truck on way to Bordeaux and tumbled Argentina over Turkey into ze brooklet beside ze road, and floated into ze proper brook and zen into ze river and into ze Bay of Biscuit. Here it tumbled and bumbled into ze churning scum at ze back of ze container ship on its way to Oz. No, Amber, it was not ze same parliamentary scum zat I told you about before.

Back at ze lily leaf, Pobble blinked, again. Ziss was quite nice, he zort, as he looked zis way, and blinked, and zat way, and blinked. Why had he not done ziss when he was a tadpole? (He didn't actually say ziss, you understand, Amber, but he would of if he could of! Zat is ze way of zings, even here in Kalgoorlie.)

Zen he noticed zat, when he blinked, ze lily pad wobbled a little. *Ziss is quite nice,* he zort, and he blinked and wobbled, blinked and wobbled. (No, Amber, I don't know whether he actually *thought* that, but I did tell you that you were not allowed to interrupret.)

Anyways, it was a very good day, he zor...never mind.

It was zo nice zat he burped. I am telling you, Amber, zat zat is what he called it, no doubt, because he was only a very new frog. If he had not been a very new frog, but an old frog, or even an older new frog, he would have known zat he had made an announcement to any frog ladies in ze same pond, or nearby, zat he was present (*present*, Amber, zair in ze pond, not *a* present...alzough...)

And, great luckiness of fire, zere *were* frog ladies in ze pond. Or, I should zay, *a* lady frog. (No, Amber, I do not know if zere is a difference between a lady frog and a woman frog—it is very dangerous for a man to zink on such matters.)

And even greater luckiness occurred as his lily pad zuddenly wobbled like ze Mayor's wife's front end that looks like ze emergency landing field for Flying Doctors when ze frill-necked lizard lost its bearings and rushed up her leg when she was inspecting ze Fimiston open cut gold mine last year, I can tell you!

Pobble didn't obzerve his great luckiness immediately, because ze lily pad had wobbled zo zuddenly and hiccuppy zat he was back under it in ze cold wet runny stuff where blinking was not an evolutionary advantage, but instinct cut in quick smart and quick smart he was back on ze lily pad and, as it happens, on ze very slinky lady frog's black and brown with a little bit of orangey warty bumpy bits but definitely not a cane toad back, where he stayed a little while.

Ziss was a time of great happiness, and it shows you, Amber, zat ze lily pad was not only ze pad of a lily but also ze froggy knocking shop.

He was now, also, Pobblebonk.

Meanwhile, far, far away, but not as far away as before, little Quercus no longer tumbled and bumbled into ze churning scum at ze back of ze container ship on its way to Oz, or wherever, because it had been swallowed by a very large killer whale zat had been chasing a not-so-large river porpoise up ze Amazon river. Ze fate of ze porpoise is not important in ziss story except to zay zat its entry into ze bowels of ze very large killer whale caused little Quercus to once again be tumbling and bumbling in ze very wet but also quite sticky stuff indeed.

You are zinking, Amber, about little Quercus, about ze cork. He bobbed and bubbed from whale to river to sea to ocean to sea to river, for years and years, seeking, searching, hoping, despairing.

Waiting for someone to zay: Put ze cork in it.

It never happened.

Zo, Pobblebonk, alone.

He liked it that way, but he was hungry.

Hungry for hamburger.

If hungry for hamburger, what do you do? You go to ze hamburger shop. Or a fish and chips shop zat sells hamburgers.

This Pobblebonk did.

Ze hamburger shop zat did not sell fish and chips was crowded, with ze crowd. Pobblebonk was too hungry to be polite, zo he hopped between all ze waiting legs and jumped onto ze hamburger-ordering counter.

Ze hamburger-cooking man in ze dirty white apron asked him what he wanted. He didn't call Pobblebonk by his name, coz he didn't know it at ze time, or even later. He hoped zat Pobblebonk would say "a hamburger with zee lot please", but Pobblebonk was too clever for zat old trick. He knew zat he had to ask for a hamburger plus each extra bit by its name—egg, bacon, lettuce, tomato, tomato sauce, fried onions, cheese slice—because doing it ze uzzer way cost ten cents more.

You may ask, Amber, how a frog can pay for a hamburger. Zimple—he pursed his lips. Ka-ching. Ha ha. Get it? *Pursed* his lips! Oh, dear, Amber, you are slow today.

Ze hamburger-cooking man in ze dirty white apron dirty-scowled at Pobblebonk, but he was trapped. By a frog!

Pobblebonk blinked twice and leapt–like ze kanga-roo–off ze counter, holding ze hamburger wiz his front foot-pads, onto the floor, dropping bits of tomato sauce on ze way, like ze wet rubies.

It was ze biggest hamburger zat Pobblebonk had ever zeen. It was giganticker zan ze biggest hamburger zat he had ever zeen. But he was hungrier zan he had ever been.

He was not like snake–he could not make his jaws go bigger–and his teeth had not been invented yet...zo! You have heard of ze lip reading, Amber–if you had been zair you would of zeen lip eating. And lip sucking.

Lip eating/lip sucking. Lip eating/lip sucking. Lip eating/lip sucking.

Ziss went on for long time. It was *very* big ham-burger, as I already told you. His eyes were not bigger than his stomach: it was ze hamburger zat was bigger than his stomach.

He lip ate and lip sucked, and lip ate and lip sucked, and ze hamburger did not get smallgiganticker, so he kept on lip eating and lip sucking and lip eating and lip sucking, and gradually ze giganticker hamburger started to small and smaller and Pobblebonk grew bigger and bigger and larger and larger until

BOOM!!!!

He exploded. Pobblebonk exploded.

Hamburger and frog and egg and bacon and lettuce and tomato and tomato sauce and fried onions and cheese slice and frog and evryzing exploded all over ze shop and ze queuing customers and ze hamburger-cooking man in ze dirty white apron, and all over and up zem and it was zo bad zat zair mothers had to throw all zair putridiculous clothes in zair incinerblasters and migrate to New Zealand or zumwear.

Pobblebonk had croaked!

And zat, Amber, is your shaggy frog story. Yes, Amber, I know zat frogs cannot really be shaggy...But I zink zat *all* stories are really shaggy...

Captain Black Jack Capes, the Gambolling Pirate

'Your Majesty,' said Captain Black Jack Capes, the gambolling pirate, winking his black-eye-patched eye lasciviously, 'at your service, re-turning with truckloads of booty from six of the Seven Seas, magnificently, munificently plundered from the boats of sixty-seven countries!'

The Queen had heard it all before, and was well aware of what went on behind this particular eyepatch.

'We are pleased to see your presence here (she paused on the second last word, to make sure that he heard the homophone). We were thinking to Ourself that perhaps Sir William was the only, ah, pirate who gave Us Proper Consideration.'

She eyed him through her lorgnette, cleverly disguised as a supercilious smile, due to the undeniable fact that the lorgnette had yet to be invented.

Captain Black Jack Capes flushed with jealousy at his rival's name, then relaxed as he remembered that Dampier had returned with no treasure from the far-south land that he pretended to have visited, but he could see, through the formerly-eyed socket, that he had failed to impress his red-haired but it must be said (but not aloud), actually balding *orange*-haired Queen.

However, he was not abashed. He was also not awashed, though clearly awake and certainly aware that he had to do better.

'And which of the Seven Seas have you *not* been to, in My Service? In clear contravention of Our last discussion.' She emphasised the Service word and the Our word, indicating, as if he needed it, the magnitude of the clear and present danger facing him, which had no requirement for visual apparatus at all.

Unfortunately, owing to his most comprehensive lack of the facility to read, and the distressing, probably litigiously impregnated oversight of the Curriculum Board of the School of Piracy in their failure to include pictograms in their lesson plans, Captain Black Jack Capes had to rely almost wholly on his memory.

'Um,' he thought.

'Your Majesty,' said Captain Black Jack Capes, a magic penny suddenly dropping from somewhere, probably a magic mint in the sky, he thought. 'Your Majesty, it's the one that I *didn't* tell you about last time!'

The Queen looked at him, directly, a Tower-of-London look, without her lorgnette (which Queens really can do without), her I-could-have-been-Henry-IX look if that bloody-sperm-had-picked-the-wrong-egg look, or whatever it was that made a chap a girl in a man's world.

Captain Black Jack Capes looked at his Queen, intuitively sure that he had noticed a Tower-of-London-head-on-the-block look, a piece of cleverness normally only residing in the females of the species, and intuitively hoping that the answer to her question was not the Dead Sea. He managed to think that that was unlikely, highly unlikely, given that it was not possible to sail there from the Adriatic Sea or the Black Sea or the Caspian Sea or the Mediterranean Sea or the Persian Gulf. Or the Arabian Sea, for that matter.

'Your Majesty,' exclaimed Captain Black Jack Capes, the gambolling pirate, gambolling joyfully around his Queen, winking his black eye-patched eye lasciviously, '*that* is why you are my Queen and not some miserable, cringing, weak-kneed, cross-eyed (he paused a moment while he considered this statement), hairless, chinless, spineless, hapless, feckless, gross-bellied, duck-billed, hey nonny-noed apology called Henry IX!'

'Ah,' breathed the Queen, 'Jackpot! Thou hast sorely tested Us tonight, Jack!'

'Neigh, Your Majesty,' replied–asserted, really– Captain Black Jack Capes, carefully removing his cape and folding it as his mother had drummed into him as an apprentice pirate, placing it under the third pillow from the left, 'my testing is only just about to begin.'

'Ah,' imperialled his Queen, putting down her lorgnette (which, of course, required absolutely no effort, a situation much-preferred by monarchs), and several other things, including her Elizabethan ruff (the homophone not escaping her), 'that is truly admirable, Admiral.'

Itches

As everyone knows, the greatest opportunity for pleasure in Creation is the itch, which is why we know that the Creator had a sense of hum-our. Or was a masochist. Or a sadist. The evidence suggests all three. However, when the matter receives the level of appreciation due to it, it becomes abundantly clear that the singular noun is only appropriate in intensely specific and personal situations—between the toes, on the calf, behind the right knee, in disparate sections (ahem), of the groin, or just about anywhere that, with a little effort, can be reached by anyone, hopefully with the scratchee's permission. The itch itself is totally insensible regarding who or

what is the scratcher. It may even have been dormant,
like Mount Vesuvius, wakened by the faintest, allegedly
accidental, touch, of a fingernail drawn lightly, uncon-
sciously, over its trillions of super-sensitive sensors,
activating billions of electro-magnetic tentacle-like
appendages, each tipped with a complex suite of
chemicals tailored to dock with the ephemeral fingernail, stimulating it and tingling the ever-in-creasing
pleasure upwards to one or other or all of the orbito-
frontal regions of the prefrontal cortex, anterior cing-
ulate cortex, and insular cortex of either or both the
scratcher's and scratchee's brains, and ending with a
climax of pleasure, pain and guilt like nothing else,
even if the itch was on one side and you were standing
in front of a mirror and scratching the other.

And an itch cannot be ignored. Once it has made
its existence known in the host's brain, by some form
of pre-emptive telepathy, no resistance is possible, a
feeble attempt at delay is not considered worthy of

attention, the die is cast, there can be no going back (depending, of course, on the location of the itch). Resistance is futile.

Criminality was an infinite itch. Criminals were the ultimate itchees. People who thought that *que sera sera* was the highest level of philosophical profundity, especially when sung. But they were also itchers, which made the whole situation as close to perfection as a detective could wish: a whole class of people who were both cause and effect.

Oscar Wilde recognised futility when he saw it, and was obviously referring to itches when he said: *The only way to get rid of temptation is to yield to it.*

Dickens intended to alert his readers to the issue, but was unknowingly frustrated in this when a slightly myopic typesetter thought Bob's name was Cratchit instead of the intended Scratchit. *A Christmas Carol* was thereby changed forever.

Ferreting with Old Mary

We were going to have rabbit casserole for tea. Actually, that's what Mum called it. I called it rabbit stew, but it still tasted good. I'm not sure what the difference is between a casserole and a stew, though we usually had a stew when we were having tea on our own and a casserole when someone was coming to visit us.

Having someone visit us was always a bit of a problem for me, because I have to get cleaned up early and put on clean clothes and then I wasn't allowed to go out and play or do anything. Dad hated having visitors the most because they were never *his* friends and he had to put on a tie and have a shave. All of these things were difficult for Dad. First of all his friends didn't usually have their meals sitting down at a table, but standing up at the bar. They knew hundreds of ways to use knives, but not with forks, and I couldn't think of any reason why Mum would have them in the house unless it was to take the carpets out for cleaning, and since we didn't have any carpets Dad's friends weren't going to come home too soon.

Visitors weren't all that bad, though. Mum always cooked something good, and too much for the grown-ups to finish.

Why we were going to have rabbit stew (we weren't having visitors) was because I was going to catch some. No, I wasn't going to catch a stew, I was going to catch some rabbits to put in it.

But right then I was having my breakfast. As it was going to be a long day I had to make sure that I had enough food in me to keep me going, so I had the same as I'd had that morning when I went around to

Miss Hendley's at Mrs Parker's to get Petchie when
Miss Hendley was fixing Petchie's legs, only instead of
having it in two breakfasts I had it all at once. I sat at
the old kitchen table, the one with the scratches and
grooves made mainly by me when I was little, before I
knew how to behave at the table. Above the table, on
the wall, was a clock which had a swinging thing hanging down from its bottom, and great big hands–a biggest one for the hours, a smaller one for the minutes,
and a third big one for the seconds, almost like the
Three Bears. One day I'm going to get a clock that has
firsts on it, instead of seconds, and then time'll go a bit
quicker when I want it to.

We'd decided to go rabbiting a long time ago, but to
do it properly takes a bit of organising, so we had to
wait for the holidays.

There are several ways of catching rabbits, some of
which are fun and some which aren't, and which I

wouldn't do unless I was starving or had no mother to get my tea.

The way we were going to catch rabbits was by ferreting.

There were quite a few of us going out that day, and each of us had to take something. My job was to take my dog Petchie, to find the rabbits. So that she wouldn't have any trouble finding them I decided that she shouldn't have any breakfast. She didn't like that idea at all, especially as she watched me eat my sixth piece of toast, but I told her it was for the best and she said that was all right then.

It's much easier talking to dogs than to sisters. Whatever you say you're doing a sister screams that you're not and that you should be doing something else that Mum said to do which you were going to do in a minute anyway but she didn't believe you. I wish sisters were more like dogs.

I thought I'd trick Mum that morning by sneaking out the back door, but she grabbed me and made me clean my teeth. It was just as well that she did, because I'd forgotten to pack my lunch. Boy, would I have been in trouble with the others if I'd turned up without it!

At last Petchie and I set off. Her broken leg and gash had healed perfectly and she didn't have to wear the kerosene tin any more. I think she was quite pleased about that but I was a bit sorry because I think it suited her.

First we had to go around to Jingo's place, to pick him up. He hadn't actually fallen down, that's just how you say it. Jingo was ready with his lunch and a bunch of tent pegs and a mallet to hit them in with so we wasted no time there. Next stop was Robbie's place, and he was ready to go, too, with his lunch and a net. The three of us then headed north towards Main Street and the railway line. Before we got there we saw

Lissie Pendle coming towards us, looking at cars' number plates and trying to remember them. She always did that when she was bored or had nobody to walk with, which was quite often as hardly anyone lived on her way to school. She had her lunch and a big billy and some matches, so the town kids were ready and off to meet the rest.

At the railway crossing we all lay down to see if we could hear any trains coming, because if we could we would've had to have jumped out of the way pretty quickly if we didn't want to have our ears cut off. I suppose you're wondering how we could see if we could hear. Well, when you've got your ear lying on the railway line your eyes are looking along it, so you can see what you can hear. We couldn't see or hear anything, so we knew that a train wasn't coming, but we all got burnt ears because the line was red hot in the sun.

Ray's house was out on the Quimbilong road, which was lucky because we had to pick up Jemmy as well. It took us about half an hour to get out there and we were as thirsty as a herd of camels by the time we walked up the gravel to the house. Ray's mum saved us all from dying or breaking in to our drink bottles by having a huge jug of homemade lemonade sitting in the Coolgardie safe ready for us. Ray was out in the home paddock rounding up Old Mary, so we sat on the verandah and soaked up the cool drink with two of the McPhee boys, who had arrived just before we did.

The verandah went right around the house, helping to keep it cool in the summer, which was nearly all the time. The verandah roof was held up by metal posts, and wrought iron hung from the top for the spiders to live in. Out the front, two big old palm trees shaded the top of the drive, and a couple of peppercorns kept the sun off the other side of the house, while the little pink berries that had fallen off onto the gravel made the drive look like a birthday cake covered in hundreds and thousands.

'How ya goin', Scratcher?'

'OK. How are you?'

'OK. How are ya, Robbie?'

'OK, thanks.'

'How ya goin', Jingo?'

'OK. How are you?'

'OK. How are ya, Pendle?'

'I'm very well, thank you. How are you, Garry?'

'OK.'

Then the other McPhee said exactly the same thing but I won't write it all out again because it's pretty boring and I don't want to give the McPhees too much space.

Just then Ray came up with Old Mary. Now I suppose that you've seen a horse. You may even think that you've seen a big horse. One or two of you might even think that you've seen the biggest horse in the world or somewhere, but if you haven't seen Old Mary then you haven't.

Each of her four feet was the size of one of our best dinner plates (the ones with the two blue birds flying over the bridge and doing soppy things in the air). She only had one toenail on each hoof, which was just as well or the road wouldn't have been wide enough for her to walk along. The front of the hoof, the naily part, was as high as a sauce-pan, and had a long hairy white fringe hanging over it. Whenever she walked in the rain she left a trail of dams behind her. The distance between her back feet and her front ones was enough space for Jingo and me to lie in, if we didn't mind being steamrollered, which we did so we didn't, but if we had've, that's how long the distance was. Looking upwards was extremely difficult and dangerous and always reminded me of that day when I climbed up the silo to get Ray's pigeons. When you looked up to Old Mary's back you first had to look up her legs, which were like hairy trees that moved. Her knees made boxing gloves seem as small as mittens, and I bet that Reverend Greensleeves and the other reverends were pleased that she never went to church and knelt in their pews.

At the back end of Old Mary was her rear, which looked like Ayer's Rock with a tail on it. The tail was huge and could've been used to hang outside our back-door to keep out the flies, which I suppose is what Old Mary used it for.

One place you *never* stood was behind Old Mary's back door, just in case she…well, in case she…sat down on you or something, or maybe swished you over with her tail.

Opposite her tail, about three miles away, was Old Mary's head, and she really needed those trees to hold it up. On top of her head were two ping pong bats, which she used to hear with and which stopped the wind blowing into your face when you were riding her, Ray said. Ray used to keep his tennis balls in there sometimes, when he didn't have any pockets. Down from the ears were the eyes, which, if you didn't have any tennis balls you could've used instead, except that Old Mary needed them and they probably wouldn't have bounced very much, anyway. Besides, they were light brown, and even in the Mallee we didn't use brown tennis balls. (This isn't exactly true, because they always went almost brown in the red dust.) Her forehead was a long, white blaze, which might have been a baby cloud if it wasn't hairy and as dry as a desert. This ended in two caves, which were her nostrils and great fly traps.

The part I liked best was her mane, which was the most important part of her because that was the bit you hung on to if you were ever able to climb onto her back to go for a ride.

I'm not sure what kind of a horse she was, but I do know that when she walked past she made breeze, so I guess that made her a draught horse.

'Who wants first ride?'

Have you ever been asked if you'd like to ride a dinosaur?

'Jingo? You want to go first?'

Jingo was looking at some magpies over in the far paddock and didn't seem to hear.

'How about you, Robbie?'

Ray was talking to thin air because Robbie had just gone to the toilet.

'Terry?'

That McPhee couldn't think of anything to say, so he pushed his brother forward.

'Oh, you want to go first, Garry. OK, hop up.'

'No, it's all right, digger. Give the young 'un a go.'

I looked at Lissie Pendle, but she was looking at me. Why was she looking at *me*? I looked at the McPhees. They were looking at me, too, including the one behind the other. I looked at Jingo. The magpies had flown away so he was able to look at me, too, now. Robbie walked around the corner from the toilet and did the same.

'Righto, Scratcher, up you go.'

'What about Liss, she's bra...I mean, she wants to have a go first.'

'It's all right, Scratcher. I'll have a go later.'

Everyone else suddenly seemed to be quite cheerful; in fact they all started to laugh and joke about different things that I didn't think were all that funny.

Petchie began to jump around and bark as Ray brought over an old wheelbarrow. He put it next to Old Mary and climbed in.

'Come on, Scratcher. Hop in.'

Before he'd said to hop *up*, now he was telling me to hop *in*. Maybe he was going to wheel me out to the rabbits.

'Now I'll bunk you up, and watch out for pigeons.'

All at once I was on top of the world. Ray and Robbie and Jingo and Lissie and the McPhees had disappeared. I could see right on to Ray's roof, and noticed the grass growing in the gutters. I could see the birds flying in and out of the palm trees, and the nests where they'd had their last lot of babies. I could just see Jemmy's place and the track leading up to it. Old Mary stood underneath me as still as could be, except for her breathing, which made me rise and fall in a happy way, and smell her warm horsey smell.

Talking about smells, what was that horrible smell coming from behind the house? I hadn't caught it before but it was wafting now into my nasal passages like an invisible cloud of poisonous gas. Someone must've dropped some old eggs into some blood and bone!

'Phew! What's that smell?!'

'What smell? I can't smell any smell.'

That was one of the McPhees. It'd take a pretty strong smell for them to smell it if either of them was around. They used to keep chook feed in their bath.

'It's coming from around the side of the house,' I said, holding on to Old Mary's mane as I looked over my shoulder.

'Oh, you must be talking about the ferrets.'

That was it! Ferrets. If you don't count the McPhees, ferrets are the smelliest things on earth. You can smell them a block away, and it doesn't matter which way the wind is blowing. I'd forgotten that we were going rabbiting by going ferreting or I would've brought a gas mask from the war. Petchie had caught a whiff, too, and raced around the back and started barking her head off. It would've been a good thing if she *had*'ve barked her head off, because then she'd have had no nose to breathe in the terrible air. It was like a mad game of table tennis—all pong and no ping.

You've probably guessed by now who had to bring the ferrets. The McPhees turned the corner of the house, carrying between them a wooden cage with a wire netting front. The smell was enough for an army of skunks but I could only see two of the little beasts sticking their pink noses through the wire. Some of the smell must've been their owners. I'm quite happy to tell you about horses and dogs and birds and trees, and even silos and Mr Braden, but if you want to know any more about a ferret you'll have to look it up in a cyclopaedia.

Ray put his haversack around his neck, passed my stuff up to me (except for Petchie, who decided to stay on the ground for now), the others picked up their things and we set off again. This was the last setting off before we really set off for the rabbits—we still had to collect Jemmy.

Old Mary dinner-plated down the drive, her reins in Ray's hands and me up somewhere near the clouds as far away from the ferrets as I could get...

We all turned up the Quimbilong road towards Jemmy's place, filling the entire space between the fences on either side of the road. The McPhees were on the left-hand side of the road, then came Ray leading the horse and me, and the rest were spread out on the right, quite a way from the ferrets. I don't think the ferrets really needed to be carried—their smell was enough to lift them along for miles.

Being on top of Old Mary was like being on top of a truck without the noise of an engine, except that the movement of her walking made my body fall all over the place at once without actually leaving her back. The view was terrific, but it was just about impossible to talk to anyone be-cause they were so far away, and the noise of four hooves crashing on the ground didn't help.

It wasn't too long before we arrived at Jemmy's farm, which was at the end of a very long track just before Five Mile Creek. On one side of the track were lots of sheep whose wool was coloured reddish brown from the dust. On the other side, scattered amongst the red gums, were a few cattle and a couple of horses, grazing on the dry grass. You'd think that they'd get sick of eating dry grass all the time, but in the Mallee they didn't have much choice for most of the time. It was a wonder the cows didn't give powdered milk.

'G'day Jemmy. You ready?'

"Course I'm ready. I've been ready since half-past five. Where've you been?'

'I had to wait for the town kids. They always sleep in till lunch time.'

'We did not! We had to get up early 'cause we had to go the furtherest.'

'Oh, yair? Well, we had to milk the cows.'

'And feed the chooks.'

'We had to feed the chooks, too.'

'But only six to ten. We've got a hundred and seventeen.'

'And we have to feed the pigs.'

That was the McPhees.

'What about the ferrets?'

'Yair, them, too.'

'What?! You fed the ferrets?! This morning?!'

'Yair, 'course we did.'

'They'll go to sleep down the burrows!'

'What?'

'Even town kids know you can't feed ferrets before you go rabbiting.'

'Yair.'

'Yair.'

'Yair.'

'Yes.'

That was the town kids.

'What'll we do?'

'We'll just have to see, won't we.'

'They're not asleep now.'

'They're not down a burrow now, either, where it's dark and not bumping around.'

Just then Jemmy's mum came out onto the verandah with a jug of cordial and a big plate of Anzac biscuits and some apricots off their trees out in the orchard.

'Here you are, boys. Oh, there's a girl, too. Here you are then. Tuck in. You must all be hungry and thirsty.'

Mrs Brister was a bustling sort of a lady. She had her hair in a bun, and a hessian apron was wrapped around her waist to keep the mess off her dress. She never seemed to walk anywhere, which was just as well with all of us to feed and water.

Because we always did what we were told we all tucked into the biscuits and apricots and drank all the cordial and Mrs Brister had to go into the kitchen three times for extra supplies. By then it was getting pretty close to lunch time so we decided that we'd better set off for the rabbits or they'd think we weren't coming.

The rabbits were still a fair way off, further up Five Mile Creek in the foothills behind Jemmy's farm. This meant quite a walk in the hot sun, but we knew it would be worth it when we caught enough for seven stews.

Lissie Pendle climbed onto the verandah railing and then on to Old Mary, Ray took up the reins, and the eleven of us were off on the final setting off before we set off for home with the rabbits after we'd caught them all. Eleven of us—one leading, five walking, one riding, one carrying the one riding (though she probably didn't know that she was carrying anyone), two being carried, and a grey one racing around everybody else, barking about an eighth stew.

Five Mile Creek was a good creek. It was much longer than five miles, Jemmy had said, that was just how far it was from Niamong where it went under the Quimbilong road. Most of the creeks around Nia-mong weren't good creeks, or if they were, they were only good in the winter when nobody cared much whether they were good or not. It was a good creek because it had water in it all year round, even when there was a drought on. There were good waterholes and a few rocky places where the water tumbled and thrushed about before landing in little pools with reeds along the banks, and sometimes bulrushes. Even on the hottest days in summer these pools were cold enough to make you think about hopping out pretty quickly, just after you'd hopped in. The only thing we couldn't do in them was dive off the bank, because you never knew whether there were rocks or tree trunks hiding under the water waiting to break your neck.

Beside one of the best waterfalls and pools was a terrific old red gum, and we'd decided to have our lunch there, and a bit of a swim.

This tree wasn't very tall, but it was big. All seven of us holding hands (Lissie made sure she held Jingo's) couldn't reach right around, and there was space inside its hollow trunk for Old Mary to stand with only her head and shoulders sticking out, and her back end. We didn't let her stay there for long, just in case her back door opened and she did something that might have made us go somewhere else to eat our lunch, so we let her lumber off to some green grass beside the creek. It's funny about big things: they don't seem to worry about things as much as little things, which didn't include her back door.

The tree had great knobbly bits all over its sloping trunk, and you could climb up on these and scale around it and jump off at different places. A couple of thin trunks which looked more like branches stuck out at the top, carrying a few handfuls of leaves to show that the tree was still alive.

As soon as Old Mary was out we all moved in to eat. When I say we all moved in to eat I meant that all the children went in, *and* Petchie and half a hundred blowflies and a battalion of ants. The ferrets were left outside, down wind, and behind a hill.

Ray lit a small fire and put the billy on to boil, and for later when we could cook our twists, then we all got out our lunches.

I had three rounds of sandwiches—plum jam, honey, and Vegemite. Jingo had three rounds of sandwiches—plum jam, egg, and Vegemite. Jemmy had three rounds, too—Vegemite, tomato, and plum jam. Lissie Pendle had two rounds of sandwiches—Vegemite and Vegemite. Ray had four rounds of thick bread and butter and—plum jam, Vegemite, and honey, and one of plum jam and Vegemite. I'm not sure what the McPhees had, but it looked like tomatoes, plum jam, honey, and Vegemite, all mixed up with a few toe nails.

After the sandwiches we had a couple of hard-boiled eggs each and some fruit—mainly apples and apricots. By then the billy was boiling and we were starting to feel a bit full, so we lay back against the inside of the tree while Ray made the tea and swung it around his head a couple of times. There's nothing quite like billy tea freshly made in the bush with water out of a good creek and swung around someone's head a few times, or even a couple of times as Ray did that day. But you have to drink it out of an enamel mug, preferably lying on your back inside a tree looking up a hollow trunk through a hole at the blue sky and sheepish clouds.

Several times during lunch I had to explain to Petchie why she wasn't having some, too, so that she would be able to find the rabbits for us easily, but I think that she disagreed with me a bit because she kept on looking hungrily at the ferrets. We all agreed that if someone looked hungrily at ferrets then it was time to go looking for rabbits.

Old Mary wasn't needed for this part, so we left her turning the creek into mud. Ray poured water on the fire to put it out. The hissing smoke sounded like one of those snakes I was talking about earlier, pouring up and out the top of the tree, making it look like a chimney.

'Come on, Petch, we're going to find rabbits!'

Petchie was off, all her woofs put away until she'd done her job, to find rabbits. She raced up the side of the creek, her nose sometimes in the air like a duchess at the Melbourne Cup, sometimes near the ground, and all the time sniffing. Suddenly she turned away from the creek and bounded up a small hill, her stumpy tail pushing her to-wards the top. I was as close behind her as you can get to a speeding bullet, and the rest panted up the hill a long way back, the ferrets bringing up the rear.

'Woof woof woof woof woof woof woof woof.'

'Coming, girl. Have you found some?'

'Woof.'

'Where are they?'

'Woof woof, woof.'

I ran in the direction she was woofing until I stopped running and started falling, my foot caught in a burrow. I landed in a lot of little round things outside another burrow and got covered in dust, but this didn't matter very much as Petchie soon licked it all off.

Looking around between licks I saw that we were almost on top of the hill. There were a few large tussocks of grass and some largish boulders, and wherever I looked there were burrows.

'Good girl. You've found some all right. Over here, everybody!'

Very soon Jingo and Jemmy and Lissie and Ray were walking around the warren, checking it all out.

'What a boomer!'

'There must be hundreds of bunnies in there!'

'Look at all those runs!'

'How many burrows do you reckon there are?'

'Must be twenty or so.'

'Are they all being used?'

'Most of them have pellets out the front.'

'I thought those were dried peas.'

'We could use them in the stew!'

'They're not going in *my* stew!'

'Scratcher fell in them!'

'I did not! I was just looking down a burrow.'

'For your cousins?!'

The McPhees had finally arrived, with *their* cousins.

'You've just arrived from *Smell*bourne I suppose.' I could say that because they hadn't got their breaths back yet and I hadn't really lost mine.

'Have we got enough nets to cover all the holes?'

Robbie pulled his net out of his bag and laid it on the ground. When he spread it out it covered an area about ten feet by twenty. Ray had two smaller nets and the McPhees had four about the same size as his. Jemmy had two small ones which looked as though they'd been used for covering fruit trees to keep the birds out.

'Let's see…that's nine. Right, spread out, everybody, and find all the holes.'

We all spread out and found all the holes. There were twenty-three, and two that had cobwebs all over them so we knew they weren't used anymore.

'We're lucky there aren't any more. We've got just enough nets. Robbie and Jingo, you put the biggest net over there, to cover those six holes.'

They spread their nets over the burrows and Lissie gave Robbie some tent pegs. He started to bang them in with Jingo's mallet but he seemed to be having trouble, missing them all the time.

'Here, give me a go,' said Jingo, 'it's a left-handed mallet.' In no time at all he had all the pegs in and the net fastened firmly to the ground.

'I'll put my nets over these holes. Give us a hand, Scratcher.'

We did another seven holes, Ray using his left hand to hit the pegs in with. Or should I say to hold the mallet with.

It didn't take long to get the rest of the nets into position, the last one being made into a kind of bag which the rabbits would run into on their way out to our dinner.

'Are we all ready?'

We all looked around and agreed that we were all ready. No bunnies would escape that day.

'OK, put down the first ferret.'

The McPhee boys started to look all proud and import-ant when Ray said this. They brought over the ferrets' cage, which they carried as though it was a palace instead of a nightman's nightmare. The rest of us stood back a bit.

One of them put his hand inside.

'Come on, Prince.'

Prince!? Prince Putrid!

He put the ferret-faced freak out by its neck and held it up for everybody to admire.

'Isn't he a beauty!?'

We all cried that he was a real beauty and that it'd be great if he was put straight down the burrows to chase out the rabbits, before he caught a chill out in the fresh air.

'Put him down that hole.'

Down that hole went Prince, to wreak havoc amongst the bunnies and make them come rushing and tumbling into our trap.

We sat down a little distance away on some rocks and waited. After waiting for a while we waited a bit longer. Then a bit longer.

'He's gone to sleep.'

'Prince wouldn't have gone to sleep. He's a champion ferret. He's caught hundreds of rabbits, and frightened millions.'

'Where is he, then?'

'He's exploring the burrows, making sure that he's not missing any.'

We waited a bit longer, watching all the burrows.

'He's gone to sleep.'

The McPhees didn't look so proud now, but they still managed to look a little important.

'Maybe he's got a bit lost. We'll send down Queenie to help.'

If they'd had another ferret I bet it would've been called Emperor, and they would've had a royal flush.

Robbie lifted up a corner of the net that Prince Putrid went under. I thought that Queenie looked a bit sleepy but I didn't say anything because the Mc-Phees had got their breaths back.

We sat on the rocks again and waited again.

'She's gone to sleep.'

'Queenie wouldn't have gone to sleep. She's a champion ferret. She's caught hundreds of rabbits.'

'Where is she, then?'

'She's rounding up the rabbits. They'll be coming charging up into the net in a second.'

They must've been rabbits without noses, to hold out for so long with those two smelly bellies crawling around their home.

I looked around while waiting for the charge of the light brigade. Behind us was a large rock, and then another, smaller one right near it. In between were lots of little bunches of grass, with bits sticking up like rabbits' ears. Like rabbits' ears!!

'They're out! They're out! The rabbits are out!'

Everyone rushed over to the hole with the loose net over it.

'No, no! Over there, between the rocks!'

Everyone rushed their eyes around to look between the rocks. About a hundred ears looked back, wiggling and furring.

'How'd they get out?!'

'They must've been blown out by the smell!'

'No! Look at Petchie!'

Petchie was nosing around the two holes that had cobwebs on them. They didn't have cobwebs on them now. And the warren didn't have any rabbits in it.

'Get them! Get some rabbits! Get some stew!'

We all rushed for the rocks and got there at the same time from different directions, crashing in to each other in a scrunchious heap. The rabbits had gone, white tails floating down the hill to somewhere else.

'What about the ferrets?'

'If the rabbits could get out the ferrets can get out.'

'I can't see them anywhere.'

'I can't *smell* them anywhere.'

'They must still be down below.'

'They're asleep. I told you they'd go to sleep as soon as they got into a dark place where it wasn't bouncing about.'

'What'll we do?'

'We'll have to smoke them out.'

'We didn't bring any smokes.'

'Not cigarettes! Smoke. Get some dry grass and twigs and some green grass. Block up all the holes except two.'

Some of us got the stuff to burn while the others put stuff in the holes to block them, then Ray lit one of Lissie's matches and put it to the dry grass. In a minute or so there was plenty of smoke and no flame so Ray placed his bag over the hole to make the smoke get sucked into the warren.

'What happens if we can't smoke them out?'

'We'll have to dig them out.'

'Wouldn't it be better to bury them?'

'We haven't got anything to dig with!'

'Then you'd better hope they...there's one!'

A coughing scrap of fur coat exploded from a hole like a cannon ball with whiskers and rolled down the hill in a mess of smoke and sneezes and rabbit pellets.

'Queenie!'

The McPhees gave chase after their beloved champion ferret, that had caught hundreds of other rabbits. Queenie thought even less of the McPhees than I did and took off in the opposite direction just as they were about to grab her, making them bang heads and fall over their boots.

'Give us a hand, will ya!'

'We're waiting for the next one.'

Smoke was still pumping into the burrows and out the other end, spreading slowly over the hillside. My eyes were starting to water a bit and Jingo coughed a couple of times.

'More green leaves. We'll make it so thick he won't even be able to smell himself!'

Jemmy and Robbie stuffed several piles of leaves on the fire and retreated to safety. The smoke billowed out the other end so quickly that we barely saw Prince leap into the air and take off after Queenie, though how he knew where she was in all that smoke I'll never know.

Then followed one of the most wonderful days of my life, watching the McPhees charging backwards and for-wards through the bitter smoke, coughing and spluttering and crashing and falling and calling the royal pair all sorts of things that weren't in the least like "Prince" or "Queenie".

'Come on, we'd better help,' said Ray, after about twenty minutes.

'Why?' said the rest of us. 'We might catch one.'

'If we don't catch them they'll go wild, and you know what happened to the rabbits.'

'They got out the burrows we didn't cover with nets.'

'No. I mean when they were first brought out from England, to breed for eating.'

Who'd want to breed ferrets for eating?

'They got away, and now we've got millions of them all over Australia!'

'Yes,' we all agreed, happily, 'so we can go rabbiting.'

Prince nicked between my legs at that moment and both the McPhees followed.

'Would there be any rabbits left if we didn't catch the ferrets?'

'There are only two of them.'

'There were only a few rabbits to start with, too.'

Queenie jumped over my face as I started to get up, and one of the McPhees splashed dust all over me as he went in chase.

'You mean they'd breed? Like rabbits?'

'Yes.'

'There'd be millions of ferrets?'

'And no rabbits.'

'Nothing but a great stink? Come on! Get those ferrets!'

We pulled the nets up and threw them into the smoke, pegs and all. Then a couple of us got on each end of a net and pulled it back out of the smoke. Jing-o and I caught one! So'd Jemmy and Liss. Hooray! A couple of yells of fright came out of the smoke and Ray pulled in the two McPhees, tangled together in the net.

'We've got the lot. We've struck the pot!'

We undid the McPhees and they unrolled the two champion rabbiters, snarling and scratching, from the nets.

'See! We said they weren't asleep.'

'Put them in the cage. We'd better be going home—it's nearly tea-time.'

Finally the ferrets were safely locked up and we did the first setting off for home, down the hill to get Old Mary. We were as tired as dogs, except Petchie, who was just dog tired. It took us twice as long to get back to the creek as it had to get up to the rabbits, even though it was all down hill.

Old Mary was lying flat on her side, her breathing making her rise like an earthquake.

'We'll ride home. It's too far to walk.'

Although it was exactly the same distance home as it was out, we all knew that Ray was right: it was too far. He coaxed Old Mary to stand up, a process which we all watched with great interest as we'd never seen a mountain stand up before. He led her over to the tree and we all scaled the trunk and hopped on her back. Ray threw the nets over behind us, between the younger kids and the McPhees. He climbed on, too, and we set off for home on the second setting-off, me holding on to Ray, Jemmy hold-ing on to me, Jingo holding on to Jemmy, Lissie Pendle hold-ing on to Jingo, and the McPhees holding on to the ferrets.

'I think we'll take a short cut,' Ray said, and he turned Old Mary off to the right, up a rise and away from the creek. It might have been a good creek, but if we were going to get home earlier then I didn't mind if we left it.

Old Mary's steady, rolling gait made me sleepy, and I could see that most of the others felt the same, especially Lissie, who had her head on Jingo's back.

We walked down through the paddocks, all the time heading for Jemmy's place, which we could just see beyond the dam in the home paddock. Over to the left the Nia-mong fire brigade was clanging its way to the smoking rabbit warren, which I thought was a waste of time as the bunnies had all gone.

Old Mary plodded on, straight for the house–and straight for the dam! Ray tried to pull the reins to one side but Old Mary wasn't going to go somewhere else, she was going to Jemmy's place, and we all went to Jemmy's place the quickest way, eleven pairs of legs wading through the muddy water–two pairs carrying, seven pairs dragging, and two grey pairs swimming behind. The only pairs that didn't get wet were the ferrets, but who cared?

Mrs Brister came out to meet us.

'How many rabbits did you get? Enough for seven stews?' Petchie barked. 'Eight stews?'

'We didn't get any.'

'None?'

'None,' we all said, except Lissie, who was still asleep.

'None?' said Mrs Brister, looking at Petchie, but this time Petchie said nothing.

She was just too sad for woofs.

Macneill of Barra

There is a small island across a black sea
Towards the sunset, westerly,
With long golden beaches, hills heather kissed,
Wide bays, still lochs, and sweet soft mist.
There lived a proud man
In castle of stone,
Loved by his clan, but
All alone.

And on that small island across the black sea,
Towards the sunset, westerly,
The lonely young chieftain wed his sweetheart:
Gold days, still nights, never apart.
There lived a proud man
In castle of stone,
Loved by his clan, yet
Still alone.

The years slowly passed, he began to despair,
When would he get his son and heir?
Then came a night's ending, goldening dawn –
From out of pain a son was born.
He was strong, he was fair,
Yes, from legends spun,
A father's prayer was
His one son.

Across their small island his son roamed so free,
His life a golden melody.
Along broad beaches, over the hills,
Jumping, running, swimming in rills.
Building a new man,
Well vers'd in life's guile,
To lead the clan in
Yet awhile.

Then away from their home, across the black sea,
The sounds of battle, stridently.
Alarums were sounded, loud was the call,
'Help us! Save us! Answer our call!'
He sharpened his sword
And hefted his shield,
Gathered his horde, all
Hearts full steeled.

They carried his body back o'er the black sea,
Along a gold path, westerly.
Back to the island home, to the old chief
Awaiting his son: grief, oh grief.
And there they were buried,
The old and the young,
Together again, and
Their song sung.

Bacon on the Menu

It was hot. Niamong was sizzling. Corrugated iron rooves shimmered in the heat and the air above the tar of Main Street looked like a mirage. Mum had all our blinds pulled down and all the curtains drawn to keep out the heat and glare. Dad kept pouring water onto the Coolgardie safe to try to keep the things inside from going bad. The ice in the icebox melted in a day and the ice man nearly melted himself keeping everyone supplied with ice.

Down in the saleyards it was even hotter. You'd think that on a day like that they'd cancel the sales and stay home, but Friday was Friday so the sales were on.

I'd decided to go down and have a look, because it was the middle of the summer holidays and I'd had bacon and eggs for breakfast and that got me thinking about pigs and that made me decide to go down and see if they were selling any that day. It's a funny thing about bacon—if you rub it around your plate hard enough at breakfast it starts to squeal like a pig, but if you rub a fried egg hard enough you just get sticky goo all over your fingers.

I climbed the high railing fence that went right around the saleyards—the part where they did the saling —and stood on the platform with the farmers and buyers and a few other kids. From up there you could see all of the pens where the stock were kept to be sold, the trucks and util-ities bringing the animals or taking them away, and the rail-way wagons waiting to load them to take them to Ballargo or Melbourne.

Peppercorn trees lined one side, along the fence where most of the people were standing, so there was a bit of shade, but the rest of the saleyards was treeless.

With all the cattle and sheep milling around, the air was like the inside of a dust storm. Quite a few pigs were already there, and the people who were going to have to shift them later were jolly lucky that it wasn't wet, or they'd never have caught them in the mud.

'G'day Mr Brister.'

'Hello, Scratcher. Caught any rabbits lately?'

'G'day Mr Phillips.'

'Mornin' Scratcher. Any ferrets got up your nose lately?'

'G'day Mr Allen.'

'I hear you might be joining the Niamong fire brigade, Scratcher.'

'Good morning Mr Rawlinnson.'

'I suppose you're sick of eating rabbit stew, Scratcher.'

It seemed a pretty good idea to stop talking to these people so I walked away, towards the pigpens. These were down towards the railway, which meant that they had been sold and were soon going to be loaded onto a goods train.

I liked pigs, especially when I was standing up on a fence looking down on them. They were so fat and hairy, and their noses looked so funny when they whuffled up and down, and their tails were so bent, that I thought they were the best animals in the world, except for dogs, that is.

I would have enjoyed being a pig, wallowing in the mud on a hot day, rooting up the ground with my strong snout, and oinking up at all the humans on the fence who only seemed to think about uncaught rabbits. On second thoughts I don't think that I'd enjoy being a pig after all, because pigs are the same as bacon, even if there aren't any eggs.

These sorts of conversations were pretty tiring. It's much easier talking to yourself, as long as you don't do it out loud. It's also a lot safer sometimes to say something in your head, especially when the person you're saying something nasty about is bigger than you and doesn't mind thumping you if you give cheek.

As I moved over towards the railway line I passed more and more pigs—there were pens filled with sows and boars (not many of those) and lots of pink piglets squealing around like lots of pink piglets. The noise was terrific, and the smell was quite interesting, too.

The saleyards were a little way outside the town, down the railway line towards Melbourne. The silo I climbed up to rescue Ray was up the line, near the station, so you know where I'm talking about. The line through Niamong was only a single track, so trains couldn't pass each other, except at stations, but the saleyards had a special siding for goods trains to pull in on market days when stock was to be transported to

Melbourne or Ballargo or somewhere. A long train stood in the siding, with about twenty cattle trucks ready for the animals. The trucks were a dirty red colour and had two floors, one on top of the other, so that more pigs could be carried at once. I don't think it would have been any fun at all being a pig on the bottom floor, but the top ones would've had a great view.

At the front of the train was the engine, a big black beast with flashes of red on its sides. It was hissing like a snake, which meant that it'd be off later in the day. If it hadn't been hissing, and if it hadn't been so hot, and if the engine driver hadn't been watching me, I'd have climbed up on top of the cabin roof and run along the boiler to the chimney, but it was hissing, and it was hot, and the engine driver was especially watching, so I decided to go for an explore along the line towards Ballargo, and maybe blow up the trestle bridge or something.

It's really interesting walking along beside a train when you're not on a platform. Everything's much bigger and you have to look up to the floor. You can see all sorts of things underneath—huge nuts and bolts, long levers, great curved metal bananas on top of the wheels for stopping the train (they were really called brakes, but I never saw a broken one), and wires of all shapes and sizes. There were even funny-looking box things over the axles, full of oil or grease, which kept dripping on to the axles to keep them shiny. I stuck my hand into one of these, to see what grease felt like: it was just like a thick, creamy jelly, or the stuff I put on my hair when I visited great-grandmother. The only trouble was that it stuck to my hand and it wasn't nice enough to lick off. Luckily there was a bunch of buffalo grass nearby, and no buffalos, and I was able to wipe most of it off on that.

There was only the goods train on the railway line that morning so I walked along the line, past the silo and station, over the level crossing on the way to Jemmy's place, and out of the town.

Walking along a railway line is fun, but a bit scary: you never know when a train is going to come along and grind you to a pulp, so it's probably best not to do it, but at Niamong we didn't have many trains. The sleepers were a little too far apart to be able to walk easily on them, so I had to do sort of walking jumps from one to the other, being careful not to let any lurking alligators snap my feet off. Petchie didn't worry much about alligators—she was still thinking about the pigs and breakfast.

It took about half an hour to get out to the trestle bridge, some of the time trudging up hill with the sweat drowning the flies on my back. The last few hundred yards to the bridge were downhill, then came the bridge, and on the other side was a long and fairly steep hill, going away from Niamong. Trains always took their time up that hill, and I sometimes wondered whether they'd make it.

When I got to the bridge I climbed down the bank and up on to one of the crossbars and looked up at the swallows. They seemed to have forgotten about the last time I was there so I worked my way up higher and sat down on the splintery wood just down from their nests. It was nice and cool, with not much sun coming through the top of the bridge and a small breeze coming off the swamp water down below. Hundreds of insects were flying around, and the swallows snapped and swallowed, snapped and swallowed, snapped and swallowed.

I wonder why swallows aren't called "snaps".

From up here you had a really good view of the swamp. Where the bridge crossed it there was a bit of running water, like a creek. In very wet weather the creek flowed quite quickly, with lots of noise and bubbles. Usually, though, there wasn't too much water and the bubbles were brown scummy froth. Further away from the bridge, on the left-hand side, was the really swampy part. Paperbark trees grew in patches of mud, tall bulrushes with brown tops and knife-edged leaves clumped all over the place in the mud, tangles of creepers snaked and twisted through the trees and bushes over the mud. Two or three huge old gums had fallen over in the mud, making causeways from one slop of mud to another. Every day was mud-day in the Great Greasy Swamp, and it was one of the best places around Niamong. The only problems were the eels and mozzies, neither of which you saw until it was too late.

Just as I was wondering what to do next I heard a whistle in the distance—the train with the pigs and cattle and sheep must have been pulling out of Nia-mong. I hadn't realised it was so late. What about my lunch? I was starving! I started to climb down from the trestle when the whistle blew again, but nearer this time. The train was go-ing to Ballargo! Over the bridge! I'd never been under a train before, or, at least, not when it'd been moving. Lunch could wait.

The whistle blew again: that must've been for the level crossing where the Ballargo road bumped over the railway line. Once when I was down there I saw old Gravyhead dozing along in his horse and cart, paying no attention to where he was, and the train blew its whistle as the cart was rumbling across the lines. The horse was half asleep, too, one minute, the next it was tearing off up the road as though it was a late starter in the Melbourne Cup. Gravyhead woke up pretty quickly then and tried to grab the reins but they'd fallen onto the horse's bottom and were jiggling around under its tail, so he couldn't steer the horse.

He started yelling then, which helped the horse go even faster. As it hit forty miles an hour the cart's front wheel hit a pothole and Gravyhead practised flying into the bank along the side of the road. By the time I got to him he'd decided to have a little sleep under the broken cart, so I set off to fetch the horse. I shouldn't have done that because it took me nearly five hours and when I got home I'd missed my tea and had to go to bed early because I'd got my shoes all dirty when I stepped in something the horse had left behind on the road when it galloped into the hills.

After a few minutes I could feel a noise coming through the bridge, so I knew that the train was getting closer.

Then I heard it puffing up the hill before the hill went down to the bridge, and then it hissed towards me, its brakes squeaking as the engine driver slowed down to cross the bridge. What he really wanted to do was to go faster, because on the other side was the steep hill that he had to climb to get out of the valley, but he wasn't allowed to as the trestle bridge was very old and it might have broken under a speeding train.

Suddenly the train was on top of me. What a noise! It sputtered and rumbled and banged. Its wheels grated and crunched and steam poured out from all sides, and a great dollop of grease fell into my hair from one of those boxes I told you about before. And then the cattle trucks ran on to the bridge and all sorts of things started falling on me. I knew that I was going to miss out on my supper again that night...and my lunch and tea.

The bridge rocked and swayed and the engine bellowed and smoked and the cattle and sheep and especially the pigs mooed and bleated and squealed and did various other things and when I thought I was going to go deaf and blind and die from the smell the whole lot had moved off the bridge and begun to try to get up the hill.

I slipped down off the trestle and started to wash off the mess, but that only spread it all over my clothes and put a bit of mud and weeds in, too. At least I would be able to get dry, as it was such a hot day, so I went back up on to the top of the bridge and sat down and waited for the sun to do its job.

By then the train was chuffing slowly up the other hill, and I could see that it was having a hard time. It was going slower and slower, and no wonder, because it was so long and all those animals must have weighed a million tons.

My back started to steam in the sun—it was really my shirt drying off, but it felt like my back. The heat was so much that I had a pretty fair idea what it must've been like to be a yabby in a saucepan getting ready to be eaten.

I began to walk back up the track towards Niamong, to see if there was any chance of lunch and to let the sun have a go at my front when...

Whhooo!!...

Near the top of the hill the train had stopped dead. No, it hadn't. It was moving backwards. Why was it doing that? Had they forgotten a load of sheep or something? The engine driver and the fireman were leaning out of their cabin, looking back at the bridge and waving their arms. I waved back. Maybe they were going to give me a ride! Lunch could wait, if I was going to get any, which I probably wasn't as I was smelling pretty badly still. Then I noticed that the fireman had climbed up onto the coal tender behind the engine and was yelling something that sounded like "Put on the steaks". They must've been hungry. You'd have thought their mums would've given them a cut lunch before they left Niamong.

I could just see the guard, sitting up on his little chair at the roof window, where he kept an eye on things. He suddenly stood up, banging his head on the roof, and disappeared from view. A second later I saw him again through the open door of the guard's van, trying to turn a big black wheel thing around. He seemed to be having some difficulty with this and the fireman began to jump up and down on the coal tender. Just then the train lurched a bit as it started to roll backwards a little faster and the fireman fell right into the tender and I lost sight of him. The engine driver was running from side to side in the cabin, twirling wheels and twisting knobs and pulling levers and blowing the whistle over and over. He must've thought I was deaf.

'Don't worry, Mister. I can hear you.'

I walked back up the other hill a bit more and stood at the side of the line, to wait. That'd be a good spot so I could hop on and they'd still be able to get a good run at the hill out of the valley. Wait till Jemmy and Jingo heard about this! I wondered if they'd mind having Petchie in the cabin as well?

Wait a minute. There's a black man in the coal tender. They must've had a stowaway on board.

Maybe that was why they were coming back, to put him off at Niamong. He seemed to be shouting, too, and doing a bit of cough-ing. Why was he wearing a fireman's overalls?

The train was going faster and faster, to be able to get up the hill to where I was standing. It clattered over the bridge and I was very glad that I wasn't under it again. I already knew what a train looked like from that angle, and felt like, and smelt like. The bridge seemed to sway a lot more than last time and I thought they'd better watch out. The engine driver was doing a bit of lairising now, showing everybody what a great driver he was, going backwards at top speed over the rails like that.

The black man was crawling over the coal tender to-wards the cabin and the guard kept leaving his wheel and staring out the door at me. I waved to him but he didn't wave back, only made some rude signs at me, so I gave him a couple back that I'd seen Dad use

at the footy a couple of times. The whistle was blowing over and over again as the train rocketed off the
bridge and started backwards up the hill towards me.

Up it came, nearer and nearer to where I was
waiting, to get on board for my ride. I wasn't quite
sure how I'd get on board when it stopped—maybe
they had a rope ladder to throw out.

They weren't stopping! A huge gust of wind and
cinders and stuff out of the cattle trucks hit me and
bowled me over and down the bank into the ditch. I
looked up and saw that the two ends of the train were
coming together as the brakes finally took hold at the
back. The train ground to a halt in a mess of steam
and screeching animals. At least, most of the train
ground to a halt, but that didn't include five of the
middle trucks, the ones full of pigs.

First one, then another, then another wobbled and
shuddered, trying to make up its mind whether to fall
over or not. The pigs inside rushed around, snorting

and grunt-ing, hamming it up for all the people who'd
stopped at the level crossing and along the road,
watching—they must've heard all the whistling.
Wobble, shudder, teeter. It looked as though the
wagons would settle back on the track until the middle
pig-mobile decided that lying down before a long
journey was better than standing up, and it fell over
with a crash like the last thunderstorm we had in
Niamong when Mr Braden opened the school fete and
we all nearly got drowned in the rain and blinded by
the lightning and everybody fell over in the homemade jams and jellies and sponges and pies and
second-hand clothes, but not the same second hand
that was on the clocks.

As the wagon crashed down to the ground the
doors splintered open and the pigs rushed out,
squealing in terror, and the other pig trucks came
crashing down, too, and all the pigs leapt out to save
their bacon. I could see the grease boxes under the

wagons bursting, and half the pigs running through the spurting grease, and then they all took off down the hill, towards the swamp.

'Stop them! Stop them! Don't let them get away!'

The engine driver and the black man threw themselves out of the engine and the guard threw himself out of the guard's van and I threw myself out of the way as hundreds of pigs charged my position. The noise was terrific as they ripped down the hill, their stumpy little legs thrashing like pistons and their tails rotating like propellers on a squadron of war-planes, making them go even faster.

The first pigs hit the swamp as a dozen men ran down the hill after them, from the parked utes and horses up on the road. The chase was on, and I was in the box seat to see the adventure. Splash! Splash! Muddy water flew into the air as the herd of swine disappeared into the swamp. Bulrushes bent over suddenly, bushes collapsed, the mud got thicker. Then men arrived and tried to catch the slippery animals. Gravyhead leapt at a huge boar, which twisted out of the way at the last second, leaving him to do his diving-into-the-mud trick. As his head came out a frog jumped off it and two piglets skittered through him, sending him back for more mud. The engine driver and the black man jumped at a passing sow which was a bit too fast for them and they fell into one of the few clean pools in the swamp. I was quite surprised to see the fireman and the engine driver come out, but no black man.

On the other side of the swamp four farmers had formed a line to stop the pigs getting away over there. They were jumping up and down and yelling to make the pigs go back. And they did. All of the three hundred wheeled round and charged straight through the middle of the swamp and into the men on this side. People flew everywhere, falling over pigs as they tried to catch them and over other people who'd already fallen over. Whenever a man grabbed a pig it wriggled out easily because of the grease and mud that was all over it. They couldn't be held—they were as slippery as eels and enjoying themselves much too much to let themselves get caught.

Up the hill they tore, towards the road and the level crossing. The whole of Niamong must've been there by then, all the ladies in their best shopping dresses and the men in their work clothes. The pigs went straight through them, scattering people left, right, and centre. I didn't know who was making more noise, the pigs running for their lives or the people falling over with grease and mud all over them, or me laughing.

Down the road went the pigs, with Petchie tearing after them, barking wildly to let all the other dogs in Niamong and twenty miles around know that they had to get into the fun pretty quickly or it'd be all over. Dogs came from everywhere and took up the chase, barking and leaping on each side of the galloping armada and biting their heels at the back. A muster from paradise, they thought.

Down the road followed the men, cursing and yelling, mud and grease covering their faces and arms and clothes.

Down the road stumbled the women, falling over their skirts and crying in rage at what the pigs had done to their shopping, which was mostly strewn across the road, a terrible temptation for some of the dogs.

Down the road after them rolled a car whose brake hadn't been put on properly, with Granny Buckland shrieking in the back.

Down the road puffed the engine driver and the fireman and the guard, their train abandoned for the day and left in disgrace for the emergency men to come and fix some time.

I ran after them all, keeping to the grass so I wouldn't step in anything I didn't want to step in.

From the top of the hill it looked like an army going into battle. The pink and grey cavalry was in front, leading the attack. They were a bit smaller than most cavalry, but just as fast and much nippier. Behind them came the infantry, brave men charging towards the enemy (in this case their own cavalry). Bringing up the rear, and streaming over a lot of ground, were the camp followers.

The battle cries could be heard from afar and I could see that the only people left in Niamong—mainly the shop-keepers—were rushing out to see what was going on.

Old Mr Grainger was there, with his son young Mr Grainger, the President of the School Council. Mrs Armstrong and her cat ran out of the Post Office and bumped into Mr and Mrs Phelpps, sending Mr Phelpps sprawling into Mrs Way and Mrs Knight.

Someone's handbag clipped Mr Phelpps's ear and he decided to see what it was like to be a four-footed animal. He shouldn't have chosen that moment to do that, really, because that was when the first pigs arrived in town...They went squealing and grunting straight over him and into the three ladies who were just trying to disentangle themselves from each other. Even the sight of Mrs Phelpps had no effect on the pigs, which had now been joined by the rest of the herd and the whole lot sped on down Main Street, leaving a trail of people and other stuff behind them.

Half a dozen men ran out of the Lalor's Arms and fell on top of the stampede, amazed and terrified at what looked like a seething, jumping, squeaking volcanic eruption. Some of them scrambled back into the pub for safety, whilst Mr Bell and the others joined everybody else after the pigs. The mess exploded through Sergeant Connally and his bike, late on the scene as usual, except when innocent small boys were concerned, and seethed past the station in a milling mass that got louder and smellier by the minute.

In the distance I could see Gravyhead prancing up and down in great excitement, thinking he was back in the war again. The whole mob raced towards him and I knew that there was going to be a greater disaster than any I'd seen before. Suddenly Gravyhead leapt aside, letting the churn-ing pigs squiffle past him in a cloud of dust and dogs–right into the saleyards, where they'd started off from in the morning. He slammed the gate onto the tails of the last little piglets and bowed to the entire population of Niamong and the train driver and the fireman and the guard. Gravyhead had saved the day!

Everybody cheered and laughed and slapped each other on the back, although I noticed that nobody actually touched Mrs Phelpps. Sergeant Connally pushed his bike over with its buckled wheels and shook Gravyhead's hand. Mr Bell brought out a great big jug of creamy soda from the pub, which Gravy-head downed in a second. Mr Grainger gave him a string of sausages, which Petchie had a good look at, and Miss Hendley gave him a kiss on the cheek–I'd have to speak to her about that later. Even Mr Braden's face seemed to be making cracking sounds as though it was trying to smile.

It was like a carnival and a circus mixed up together. Behind the gate the pigs were milling around the pen, waiting for the sale to begin again and in the meantime getting their breaths back and digging up the ground with their whiffling snouts. Outside, the crowd was moving away from the saleyards back into the main street and Mr Bell's hotel, being careful where they stood.

The engine driver and his fireman and guard began to trudge back to their train, and I headed off home.

For more bacon and eggs, and maybe a bit of ham or pork if there was any.

Like a Man

*[The Malay Emergency, 1948/60, was the attempt by Chinese
Communist 'terrorists' to end British rule of the country.]*

'Come out and fight like a man.'

Mac showed the note to Nair.

'It's a trap, obviously,' his 2-i-C said. 'They can't get at us here, so they want us to go to them.'

Mac had no doubt that that was the intention, and also that it was highly unlikely that Nair would put himself in any more harm's way than he was at present —that was definitely not part of his job description.

The *Emergency* was in its fifth year–quite a period for an "emergency"–more like a war–but there were many reasons why the British Cabinet didn't want the situation to be called a war–none of which impressed the two men in the middle of the situation.

Seventy-five had died so far, Nightingale only the day before, at Teluk Anson. Nothing like up the line on the Railway, but death is death and should be attended to, hang what they thought in Whitehall.

Night-time almost always meant the sound of rifles in the distance. The near distance. He was a little puzzled as to why they seemed never to kill the coolies–the Special Constables who went out with them couldn't be everywhere. Maybe they intimidated the rubber tappers in order to get information, or food. He should have thought of that. He'd always seen the Tamils as being loyal to him, but loyalty can become a little shaky when a gun is touching your throat and the threats are delivered in a language that has nothing to do with world peace.

The note was signed: *The People's Fang.*

'Melodramatic!'

'Yes, Mac, but not toothless?'

It was the first time he'd heard Nair crack a joke, but neither man laughed.

'Has any war been won by defending? Or by retreating, even to an impregnable fortress?' Mac had done both—in Singapore and on the Siam-Burma Railway—and knew *an* answer that had worked, at enormous cost and over much time. 'Who is stronger, an attacker or a defender?'

Unlike some of his ancestors from Kerala, Nair didn't have a military background, and tended to keep his own counsel.

'What would our workers think, Nair? Do they want us to just sit here, safe in our compound, our

"impregnable fortress", double fences, floodlights?'
Most of the workers were Tamils, who'd never been
consulted about anything. 'They would want to be
safe.'

'You've already risked your life, and the SCs'. We
are safe here.'

'*Are we?* The coolies are out in the plantation every
day—men and women. We can't protect them when
they're tapping or collecting. We're essentially protect-
ing only ourselves! That isn't right. And it won't win
us the war.'

His decision to build the double fence around the
bungalow, factory, and workers' living quarters had
proved its value—the CTs didn't like the flood lights
and the barbed wire.

He'd had a Mercury car since last year, completely
covered in armour plate, and a GMC Light Reconnais-
sance Car was on its way from England. A fully-

armoured Ford V8–nearly three tons–was due in a few days. A police station was three miles away and another eight miles the other way. A shotgun was with him day and night and a policeman was always on guard. On top of that he had two of his own men on guard around the house, with shotguns, and Nooradin, his personal bodyguard (who stuck to him like a leach!). There were also fifty Malay and Indian Special Constables, and, as an Honorary Police Inspector, he had access to up-to-date intelligence. Army units camped downstairs from time to time, including Ghurkhas, and he had supplied two shotguns to the *fau cheung*[3] at Tanjong Tualang to help protect the village.

'Who is this *People's Fang*? A new kid on the block?'

It was a rhetorical question: Nair, being a Tamil, didn't have access to Chinese goings-on, and didn't really want to. He wished privately that Malaya, like India, had the Himalayan Mountains between the two

---

[3] Village headman.

countries, though he was very friendly with Cook. Nair admired both the English and the Scots, and the Australians at a pinch, and he could see where his employer was leading.

'He needs a show!'

The lorry pulled up at the edge of the plantation, just off the Batu Gajah road, Mac's armoured V8 reversing into a spot nearby, facing the road. He stepped out of the safety, scanning the jungle, Nooradin coming a-round to join him, Sten gun ready.

Asad and Haaziq climbed down from the cabin, rifle safety catches off. Aamil remained in the lorry, with the walkie-talkie. They were to remain with the vehicle, to guard it and as back-up.

Mac checked the others, carefully but confidently—these were the pick of his SCs. Altogether, his twelve best men. Thirteen, counting himself, but he wasn't superstitious. Not, that is, apart from insisting that they always lined up in alphabetical order. He had recruited each of his Special Constables, choosing men whose given names seemed to him to be auspicious—Aamil (workman), Aashif (bold, courageous), Aiman (fearless), Asad (happy, lucky), Falah (success), Ghazi (conqueror), Haaziq (intelligent, skilful), Haytham (young hawk), Jabr (mighty, brave), Mahdi (guided to the right path), and Zubair (strong, smart). These had been with him the longest and had proved to be the most reliable. He had been tempted to call them the Twelve Disciples, but Twiggy would surely have said that "Apostles" was preferred.

All were dressed similarly, in loose, grey-green fatigues, floppy hats almost concealing a degree of nervousness. Heading into an operation—soldier or surgeon—required nervousness. Too much confidence might spell death for the one with the gun, or the other under the anaesthetic (if there was one, Weary);

too little—faint heart doesn't win fair lassie. Better to be sure than sorry, but how could you be sure in either situation?

'Mahdi.' The young man stepped out of the line, un-slinging his rifle. Mac jerked his head towards the path. 'Let's go.'

Mahdi released his safety catch and padded away, quickly disappearing into the perimeter path. He loved being the leader, out in front of the older men, and know-ing that the magic talisman hanging around his neck would certainly deflect any bullets fired at him. The merest graze on his shoulder was conclusive evidence of this, coupled with the impeccable reputation of the dealer he'd bought it from.

Satu, dua, tiga, empat, lima...sembilan belas, dua puluh—

Twenty seconds. Aashif followed, then Aiman, Falah, and Ghazi at twenty-second intervals. Mac always counted in Malay, the first words he'd learned on the job.

He followed as Ghazi slipped out of sight, nodding at the others standing beside the truck, soon becoming dappled under the shifting clouds, lightly fingering the butt of his revolver. The last thing he saw was Aamil turning the lorry around, positioning it beside the Ford.

The old tingles ran down his spine, somehow dissipating into the soft ground. His boots made no sound, save for the occasional muted crack when he stepped on a rotting twig. The plantation on the right was quiet—it often was—and the jungle to the left was much the same, though this was definitely not normal. Even the brooklet seemed to be keeping its own counsel. Was the noiselessness because of him and his men, or for a more sinister reason? Possibly, though he'd never seen one in the wild, a Panthera tigris?

That would be interesting! He hadn't thought about that before, in what he called his "patrol musings", when he was habitually in two minds—one thinking about just about anything, the other focused intently on the environment and potential threats.

The creek pushed the path away from the plantation, rising slightly, keeping pace with its twists and diamond-studded stoneware. He had a vague sense of a troop of Macaques somewhere in the far distance, but that barely intruded on the silence. He glanced behind him—Nooradin came into sight—*he* hadn't counted to twenty!—and cursed as he stumbled on a root. Breathing was easier in the cooler air, the unseen eddies cooling his sweat-soaked shirt, but not drying it.

Then all went cold: his body, his brain, his heart.

The small star that gave life to everything splashed its ninety-three million miles impartial heat and light down on a large clearing, on his forward men, on a giant oak larger than any he'd seen at Home.

Onto a body, swinging gently from a giant branch reaching imperiously across the clearing.

'CUT HIM DOWN!'

Jabr grabbed the body. Falah whipped his *kris* from its sheath and slashed and slashed the jute twine, and both gently lowered the body to the turf. Haytham looked everywhere else, wary, nerves taut.

Mac looked at the body. 'It's *Deepak.*' *"Lamp" or "light"—he was in the last batch of Tamils brought over before the war. My boys played with his boys. When?* He hadn't heard that anyone was missing. Must have been this morning. *Are they still here?* 'Falah, Jabr—get him back! Aashif, Zubair—go with them. Tell Batu Gajah!'

Less than half the patrol remaining in the clearing. Go on or go back? Attack or defend? *Are we men, or are we not?* Deepak had a wife and three children. *My men have families—can I risk their lives when the risk is so real?*

He fell, the pain in his leg excruciating. Aiman fell, screaming. Falah dropped, his rifle slapping uselessly into the grass. Ghazi ran, rifle pointing upwards, and fell. Mahdi fell, across the path, his last path. Haytham fell, looking up into the trees. Sten gun bullets seared through the lantana bushes leaning out of the jungle, exploding their red and blue and pink and orange and yellow flowers in rainbow starbursts. Chen Choo's flowers.

'Tai luk mou,[4] kwy loh[5]!'

White man kicked, weapons seized, talisman ripped off. Independence one step closer.

Macaques whooping across the glade, long tails grace-fully demonstrating the wonders of evolution.

...*like sitting ducks*, wrote the young Captain of the Worcestershire Regiment, to his mother.

---

[4] Wearing a green hut: a cuckold.
[5] A highly derogatory term for a white man.

Your Grandfather

'Yer like a kookaburra tryin' to swallow a rock python! Tryin' to tuck in and the snake's rear end's holdin' onto a sapling for dear life, or maybe its own dinner, and swingin' the kooka round and round like a bullroarer, feathers flyin' everywhere, 'n' the snake lookin' at the back of kooka's stomach 'n' not carin' which way was up! You never let up! Even with yer mouth full ya never let up!' She looked at the girl. 'All right, then. How many birthdays 'ave ya had?'

Merry held up both hands, fingers and thumbs illustrating the situation.

'Wonders never cease!' Flo had seen many wonders, most that she liked to forget. 'All right, pet, next time you'll need your toes as well, ay. Why not? S'pose it's time; can't do any harm.'

The old lady pushed a log further into the fire, watching a spider rush out of the cool end and tiptoe helter-skelter across the red dirt into the scrub. She looked away, to where she'd never been, but where her ancestors had come from, so long, long ago, from where the sun stood high at all those noontimes. She seemed to settle, and grow, and disappear.

The child looked at her grandmother. *If the fire goes out I won't be able to see her.* She tilted her face up. *And if the stars go out I won't be able to see the sky.*

Slowly, comfortably, Flo's English left her.

'Your mother was my last. She was born on the very day that Menzies declared war on the Germans.

Menzies seemed to like declaring war on someone! He did it again, Korea. The Kiwis would've been next!'

The universe was possibly a little upset with this possibility, and didn't let it happen.

'Your grandfather was a great man. We had a good life. Although he came from another country he loved it here, especially the horses. We couldn't send your mum or the others to school because there wasn't one anywhere near, but that didn't matter. I taught them all about the bush, and my songs, and Dad taught them about other places, other things. The kids played in the creek, or fished in it in the Wet, Dad getting into just as much trouble as they did, when he wasn't away, working on a station. He always sent money back, and brought you books and things. We were happy, though I suppose we didn't think about it.

'Then the war came.'

A very long pause; the warm night waiting.

'Your grandfather thought he had to help out. He saddled up when your mother was four months old...

'Somehow I got a letter from him before he sailed. He'd joined something called the 8th Division. He was a machine gunner. I didn't know what those things were. Still don't. Didn't say where he was going...'

The child had no experience of grandfathers, or fathers for that matter, and only one grandmother. What grandmothers thought about grandfathers had no place in her mind.

'There was just one problem, which hadn't been a problem while he was here. The Welfare.'

The child's mother seemed to tighten, leaning back from the light. 'The *Welfare.*'

'The Welfare. That's what it was called. You didn't see him again till you was six. Too late. Wrong time.'

Time: it knows nothing. Not out here, near the desert. Not when it rains and the frogs begin their wrestling journeys through the mud up to the light. Not when the dry creeks flood into new/old great lakes. Not when the bird masses massed in the new/old fishing grounds, feeding and breeding; breeding sometimes till it was too late.

'He couldn't ride a horse; couldn't ride a horse anymore .'

Time can wait. It waited.

'He was…different. Turned out he went to Singapore…'

> *Singapore. Off the ships. Too late. Deployed to the north of the island. Japs coming. Australia Day. Brits, Indians, volunteers, the 8th—all retreating. Said they would never invade from the north—jungle. Bombing getting worse. Our mob tracking back across the causeway. Hundreds. Japs riding bikes through rubber plantations.*

We should've had bikes! Causeway blown up. Safe? Bombing worse. Shelling. They can see us from the palace. Singapore island. Island. *Gallipoli? Eat. Watch. Shadows on shadows.* Barges! *In range? Fire! Fire! Fire! All night. Ten thousand rounds. Barrel glowing. Mates' barrels glowing; ten thousand rounds each. Trying to kill...twenty thousand. A million. Shouting. Screaming. Outflanked. Fall back! Fall back! Fight. Fighting. Fighting. Still alive. Fighting. Exhausted. Exhausted. Island. White flag. Changi.*

Chinese massacred. Bayonetted. Beheaded. Thousands. Thousands. *What'd they done? Heads on stakes. They were Chinese.*

Rice. Concerts. Sport. Japs couldn't care less. Couldn't last. Forty thousand marched to Selerang. Dying. Mates shot— wouldn't sign won't escape document. Teaspoon of meat twice a week, if you worked—had to keep the Japs fed.

Farewell, Singapore! Holiday Camp!

Railway. Steel trucks. Ovens. Four days. Cooked sardines. Siam. Bam Pong. March. March. March. Three weeks marching. Dying. Monsoon all day, all night. Mud knee high. March, march, march. Jungle. Dying. Flo. Rain. Kinsaiyok. The boys. Kannyu. Splitting rocks. Speedo! Speedo! Eating mud. Duck eggs! Chungkai. Beatings. Snaring lizards. Kempeitai. Dying. Nakhon Pathom. Poor bloody Tamils. Kitty. "Hospitals". No clothes. No blankets.

Freezing cold. Dying.   Digging graves.
Saint   Weary.   Weary   saint.
Kanchanaburi. Japs losing. "Liquidate all
prisoners." Mushroom bombs...

'They found him down by the billabong. Yair, under a coolabah tree. With the rope.'

Beginnings and Endings

How did it happen? How could it have happened? She wasn't allowed to roam the streets–she always stayed out the back or in the house.

It couldn't have happened when we were taking her for a walk, because we would have seen it happen, even if it had been terribly embarrassing.

Brissy was going to have pups.

She was starting to get fat. Not the same way as Mum did before she had Bill, but sort of *droopy* fat.

Her tummy seemed to fall down, with little knobs on it, but I wasn't sure what they were. I thought they might've been the new puppies' toes or something.

The thing was that we didn't have a father dog, and without a father dog it's impossible to have a mother dog,

I think. Our house had a fence all the way around it, nearly as high as me in the front, and higher everywhere else, so that any dogs who thought they might like to be-come father dogs would have an uphill battle–and we were keeping a sharp watch out.

We had heard a few noises, but that was probably possums, especially as it only happened at night. And sometimes we noticed a bit of mud on top of the fence, but that was probably Bill, so we really didn't know about the puppies until they were almost born.

It's no good having a father who's a doctor when your dog's having puppies–you need a vet. Vets do almost the same training at the university as doctors do, but doctors don't do almost the same as the vets. I could never imagine Dad asking Brissy to poke her tongue out. The only trouble was—we didn't really know that Brissy was having pups until it was almost too late. I think Mum and Dad were a little suspicious about the noises at night, and the mud on the fence, but because they never actually *saw* a father dog anywhere near Brissy they didn't worry, although they did talk about it sometimes.

Then one night, about the time when the nightmares are galloping through my head and around the room, I heard Dad leap out of bed and crash into their bedroom door, which he'd forgotten he'd closed so that the light wouldn't stop me going to sleep while they were reading. He yelled something and light fell into the passage and onto me. It didn't really hurt me, because it was quite light, but it certainly woke me up pretty quickly.

'What's happening, Dad?! Is the house burning down?'

'No! I heard a scrabbling under the house! I think it's Brissy!'

'Is she burying a bone or digging one up?'

'No! I think she's having pups!'

I thought *Dad* was having pups, the way he was carrying on.

'Why's she having them under the house? Why doesn't she go down to the hospital? Like Mum did.'

'*She* wasn't having pups!' said Dad, trying to get his left arm into the right sleeve of his dressing gown.

I thought that I'd better not say anything about that. He did up the cord at the back and rushed down the passage to the back door. He looked as though he was going in three directions at the same time, because he had his slippers on the wrong feet.

'Wait for me! I'm coming!'

In a second or two my dressing gown was on and my slippers were on, and my torch was on–because it was dark out there. I hurried down the passage to the back door, so that I wouldn't be too late, just in time to be knocked over as Dad came charging back in.

'My torch! My torch! I need a torch!'

Looking up at him from the floor I wondered if he was always like this when he was delivering babies. He probably sent the *fathers* into the room while he paced up and down outside.

'I've got a torch,' I said. 'It's a good bright one.'

'Come on, then!' he yelled, pulling the torch out of my hand and disappearing through the door.

I climbed off the floor and went out the back, following the light of the torch as it fell through the plumbago and strawberries.

By the time I'd reached the side of the house Dad had already climbed through the access door and was scuffling through the dust towards the front of the house, banging his head on the floor every few seconds.

(Under a house is the only place I know where you can bang your head on the floor when you move your head upwards, unless you're lying on your back, of course.)

'Hello, girl!' I heard Dad yell softly. 'How are you?'

Dust splashed into his face as her hairy tail whacked the earth, making him sneeze and bang his head again.

'There, there, girl. Are we having puppies?'

I *knew* we should've got the vet.

Brissy's great brown eyes looked at us, but she kept moving her head around, and sniffing. She didn't seem to know what was going on. She must've gone to the same medical school as Dad. She kept on getting up and twisting round and round, and lying down and getting up again.

'What's she doing, Dad?'

'I think she's trying to make a nest for her pups.'

'How can she make a nest without any feathers?!'

'They usually make a nest in the grass, a kind of snug place for the puppies to keep warm in.'

'Where are the puppies?' I thought they must be still inside her, because I could still see their toes sticking out.

'They're not ready to come out yet. She's just getting ready for them.'

'Why don't we bring her inside?'

'It's probably best not to disturb her. Come on, I think we'll go back to bed.'

We gave her a pat each, but she didn't seem to be interested. I don't even think she realised that pat was tap spelt backwards, either, but why should she when she was about to have a pup, which was the same backwards *and* forwards.

'You hop back into bed, Liss. I'll call you if anything happens.'

'All right, but I'll never go to sleep while Brissy's having pups.'

'Wake up!' shouted a voice crashing down the passage.

The sun was just coming up over the town, making the magpies sing about their breakfast and the crows tell us what Noah built in the bible. Frost covered the front lawn, the chooks out the back started to kerk, and the old rooster crowed a couple of times, which is what the crows should've done.

'One's out! One's out!' shouted the floor under my feet, so I raced out the back and around the side, even though it's pretty hard to imagine a round side.

'She's trying to bury it!' shrieked a voice between the stumps, and I heard Dad bang his head on the floor again.

The space under the floor looked like the Showgrounds the day I went for that ride on EG IV, the giant prize bull–dust was everywhere.

'Go and tell Mum that I'm bringing her into the laundry!'

I left him trying to find the pup that was buried and told Mum the good news about the laundry, but she'd heard it all through the floor.

Newspapers were everywhere. In the corner was an old suitcase, with the lid open and propped back against the wall. Inside the case she'd put some straw and bits of crumpled-up paper. And she'd put the kettle on.

'Go and tell Dad it's all ready.'

Back under the house I went, with a handkerchief over my mouth and nose for the dust.

'What have you got that on for?' dusted Dad.

'You have to wear a mask when babies are being born. You should know that.'

'What did you bring the spade for?'

'To dig up the puppy she buried.'

Oh for a vet. Didn't he know anything about animals?!

'Is Mum ready yet? Why's she taking so long?'

'She was ready before you asked her.'

'Oh.'

I supposed P would come next. Little did I know.

Dad carried Brissy into the laundry and put her into the suitcase, and went back for the buried treasure.

Brissy didn't look terribly sure about what was going on, which was fair enough, I suppose, as it was her first set of babies. She kept turning around and looking between her back legs, and licking herself, and looking up at us.

'Look! Look! One's coming!'

Her tummy was moving around a bit, and then, suddenly, a long shining thing plopped out from between her legs. She looked at it, not knowing what to do.

'Lick it!'

Brissy looked at Dad and licked her lips.

'The puppy! Your baby! Lick it! Lick it! Lick it!' shouted Dad quietly again. I thought Brissy had the right idea the first time. Who'd want to lick *that* slimy mess? Even to see what was inside.

She looked at the slightly wriggling thing at her back end.

She sniffed it.

And she started licking it.

'Good girl!' purred Dad. 'You're a very good girl! What a clever girl you are.'

I thought she was stupid. Slurp slurp slurp. It was revolting. And then she ate what shed licked off! She ate it!! Yurkk!!

And there was the most beautiful little animal you've ever seen in your life!

It was black, all over. Its eyes were shut tight, screwed up in its wonderful black face. Brissy licked it and licked it in great doggy kisses, telling it that she loved it, even though she didn't know it very well yet. It lay there, lapping it up, getting its strength to crawl over to have its breakfast. Then it mewed like a kitten and nuzzled into Brissy's tummy.

'How many puppies will she have, Dad?'

'I don't know, really. Perhaps seven or eight.'

Seven or eight!

'Here comes another one!'

Another flat wet balloon appeared. Brissy didn't waste much time getting off the slimy stuff so that it could have its breakfast, too. It was as black as the first one.

'They do look rather like Labradors, dear,' said Mum.

'Yes, they do. But we couldn't be that lucky could we?'

I didn't know what they were talking about, but I did see the next slug before they did. That made three black ones sucking at Brissy's tummy.

'Here's Number Four!'

'Number Five!'

'Number Six! Number Six is a white one!'

It was like the top of the milk—white but not quite white. And it was even more beautiful than the others, although I wouldn't have told them that. She looked just like Brissy.

It scrambled over to its mother and pushed its way

into the middle of the others, so that there were black ones on each side, and it started pulling away at Brissy's drinking fountains. The other four had bellies like balls and they'd more or less stopped drinking.

Number Seven was a white one, too.

'Seven,' said Dad. 'I think that'll be all.'

We sat at the kitchen table and watched our new family through the laundry door. Mum and Dad had a cup of tea, Dad rubbing his head a bit as he drank.

'What're we going to do with them, Dad?'

'I think they'll be all right in the laundry for a while,' said Dad.

'No, I meant when they get bigger.'

'Dad can make a run for them out the back. But we can't keep them, dear.'

'Why not? They're lovely!'

'Yes, but they grow up, and I'm not having eight dogs running around.'

'Nine. There's the one Brissy buried.'

'I'm afraid that one didn't make it, Liss. I think it must've been a little weak,' said Dad quietly. 'I didn't get to it in time.'

I was sad when he said that. Poor little thing. Then I noticed Brissy moving around in the suitcase.

'Dad! I think she's having some more!'

'She couldn't be!' said Dad, not quietly.

But she was. She had four more: two black ones and two white ones. How'd they all get a drink? I didn't think that she had enough taps.

'We might have to help her, with a bottle,' Dad said, even though I hadn't said anything out loud. But Brissy thought that that would be quite unnecessary.

The rest of that day I stayed in the laundry,

watching the fluffy little things sleeping and drinking, and wriggling into a good spot for a drink, and then going to sleep with their little black noses snuffling against Brissy's tummy. Some-times she'd get up and turn around and they'd all fall off and I'd have to put them back. They always woke up when they fell off, and discovered that they were hungry again so they had to start tugging at the milk supply again.

One day their eyes opened, all of them on the same day, even the littlest. By then there were nine pups left. I don't think she had enough milk for twelve, or she might have accidentally squashed them at night, but the nine were really healthy and strong, waddling around just about on their fat tummies. Brissy seemed to be quite proud of them and I thought they looked lovely, the three white ones falling over the black ones, playing happily as they grew bigger.

We still had newspaper all over the floor, because they didn't know about the garden and what dogs are supposed to use the garden for, and Mum had to ask some of her friends for extra supplies. The bigger they grew the more layers of paper we had to put on the floor, and we had to keep on changing it.

I wanted to keep all the pups for ever, but after they were about ten weeks old Mum and Dad started finding good homes for them, and soon we were back to only Brissy. I didn't think she minded all that much by then because I think she was getting a bit tired of being chased and bitten and sucked, but I missed them.

Mum and Dad talked about having a spade for Brissy so she wouldn't have any more pups and she went off to the vet for a couple of days. I didn't see why she couldn't have had our spade.

All that happened years before. Brissy never had any more pups, which just goes to show that spades are useful for other things besides digging up the garden. We did meet the father of the pups, though.

He was a new dog who'd moved into Niamong not long before and who lived down near Jingo's place. And he was a Labrador! A black one, so that explained all the black pups and why they looked like Brissy, even though she was white.

I taught her to sit and lie, and to fetch a stick, and Bill taught her to bark when he came along. When I came home from school she'd be waiting for me at the gate, panting, and wagging her tail. We'd go for walks along the creek, and swim in the summer, her strong legs pulling her through the water nearly as quickly as I could swim. If I didn't watch out her long claws would scratch me, because when she was in the water she couldn't stop swimming, even when I was holding her.

And now she was old.

She'd stopped getting fatter a while ago, and started getting thinner. The whiskers along the sides of her mouth turned white, and after she met me at the gate we took a long time getting back up the hill to the house. The rabbits in the paddocks up the back became lazy and cheeky, hardly bothering to run away when we went for a walk up there, and she stayed pretty close to the track I was walking along.

Bill thought it was very funny when she fell over, or couldn't get up properly when she was lying down, and we all laughed a bit. Dad said she was getting arthritis, which made her joints stick.

One day Dad took her down to the vet. When he brought her home he said that the vet'd given her some tablets for the arthritis, to see if they would help. He said her heart was pretty good for a dog her age, even though it was a bit wonky. We crushed a tablet into her meal each night, and fussed over her to help her get better. She wagged her tail and licked us.

But she didn't get better and she didn't really eat her food. One day she couldn't stand up at all.

Mum and Dad were very quiet. I stroked her head and talked to her about her lovely puppies, and Bill tried to get her to drink some milk. She lapped up a few drops and licked a milky tongue over his fingers, and laid her head back tiredly on her rug.

'I think I'll take her back to Dr Hilton,' said Dad.

He picked her up gently, cradling her in his arms like a baby. Mum went off to her room.

'Give her a pat, son,' said Dad. 'Liss.'

We stroked the old girl down the passage.

'How long will she be down at the vet's, Dad?' asked Bill.

'I don't know. I'll see.'

He put her on the back seat of the car and drove slowly away down the hill.

Ranga Meets God

'Would Ranga from India please report to the Purser's office. Would Ranga from India please report to the Purser's office.'

Western Australia was far behind. *Strathnaver* was moored at Port Adelaide. The public address system blared throughout the ship, down below reverberating along passageways, on deck being whisked around and away by the warm wind blowing from the shore. Ranga was leaning over the rails, watching the traffic on the wharf, and the people leaving the ship down the gangway. He was quite excited, seeing this next part of Australia, and a little relieved that he hadn't been bitten in the Great Australian Bight, where most of his friends had been leaning over the rails for a different reason, mainly to do with feeding the fishes.

'Would Ranga from India please report to the Purser's office. Ranga from India, please report to the Purser's office.'

'Ranga!' Teacher Kumar had come up behind him. 'Ranga! They're calling you! Are you sleeping on this fine Australian Saturday!?'

Of course he wasn't sleeping! He was *think*ing! The Captain of India had to think, or everyone would be let down!

'Come with me; I will accompany you to the Purser's office!'

They left the rail and stepped over the door sill into the corridor leading to the Purser's office. Deputy Purser Cockle was waiting for them.

'Ah, there you are, Ranga! I thought that we would have to send out a search party! We have a little surprise for you.'

He took Ranga's elbow and led him down the passage and back out onto B Deck. 'Yes, Kumar, come along, too!'

They walked past the first gangway, then the second, heading towards the First Class section. Ranga's interest rose, catching glimpses of the expensive cabins through the large porthole windows.

'Where are we going?'

'You'll see.'

It was very mysterious, which Ranga enjoyed, and he could see that Mr Kumar was just as intrigued.

They finally turned inside again, and then up some stairs to another passageway (where there were no passengers), just a couple of crew and a steward about to carry a tray into a cabin.

Mr Cockle stopped him.

'Please inform the Captain of the *Strathnaver* that the Captain of India is here.'

The Captain of the *Strathnaver*! Ranga gulped, and he was quite sure that Kumar did the same. They both stood, shaking slightly, beside Deputy Purser Cockle as the steward nodded, knocked on the door and carried his important wares through to the Captain's inner sanctum.

A thousand years passed as two sets of dark eyes glued themselves to the closed door, and one amused set of blue eyes watched them, anticipating the final execution of his surprise, which wasn't really his, anyway, but it's always good to be in on something good.

I'm going to meet the Captain! thought Ranga. *Oh, wait until Harkishen hears about this! And wait until Appa and Amma hear about this! And wait until Ajji and Ajja hear about this! And the other Ajji and Ajja! And all my aunts and uncles and cousins hear about this! And wait until...!*

It was quite amazing how many people were going to hear about this, and all being thought about in less than a thousand years, but the Captain's Day Room door was suddenly opened and there stood the Captain of the *Strathnaver*, in his immaculate white uniform, with so much starch that it actually crackled!!

'Ranga? Ah! Ranga! I am so pleased that you could come!'

Come?!

'It is very good of you to spare the time.'

Spare the time!? These English were certainly very strange, but Ranga certainly had no trouble understanding him.

Unfortunately, just at that moment, although it had probably also been the case for the previous thousand years, Ranga was unable to speak.

But a person does not become the Captain of the *Strathnaver* without knowing about these things, even though he had spent nearly all his life at sea, and nearly all of that time P&Oing.

'I see that you found your young, Cockle. Well, please come into my cabin.'

Captain Mellonie gently took Ranga's arm and guided him into…a palace! Beautiful chairs and sofas were placed around a low table, which Ranga could see was fixed to the floor, but this was not important. Lovely pictures adorned the walls, mainly of olden days ships, but this was not important. On the floor was a rich, soft, maroon carpet, which tickled his bare feet quite pleasantly, but this was not important. He was in the presence of the Captain of the *Strathnaver*! *That* was important!

'Now, young man, I have someone here to meet you.'

Someone to meet him? Ranga thought that he was meeting the Captain of the *RMS Strathnaver*! He hadn't noticed the man sitting in a big chair near the window, who now stood up and walked over to him, smiling.

'Good morning, Ranga, I am so pleased to meet the young Captain of India!'

Ranga turned to this person, who had slightly receding hair, and whose hand was reaching out to take his.

'I'm Donald Bradman.'

!?!!?!!! ?!!!!?!!!!!?!!!!!!?!!!!!! ?!!!?!!?!!!!!!!?!!!!?!!!?!!!!!!!!!! ?!!!!!!!!!!!!!

The walls fell in.

The pictures fell off the walls.

The carpet disappeared in a puff of smoke.

The chairs crashed into each other.

The ship probably sank.

'Ranga! Aren't you well??!'

Well?!?! *Wait until Harkishen Singh hears about this! And Appa and Amma! And Ajji and Ajja! And the other Ajji and Ajja! And all my aunts and uncles and cousins! Not to mention Harkishen Singh* rushed through Ranga's mind, even though he'd already mentioned his guru at the beginning of the thought.

He took the great man's hand, trembling, the hand that had held so many bats and made so many runs, and could even bowl leg breaks, which he himself could do, sometimes, but not at the same time.

'Your letter found me! As I recall, it was addressed "Bradman sir, Australia". Unfortunately your letter did not have *your* address, so I could not reply to you!'

How could he have doubted the great man!!?

'So I just had to keep my ears open, to see if anyone from India had found his way into Australian waters. And, fortunately, I have many friends in P&O...'

Ranga looked around. Captain Mellonie was smiling and nodding. Kumar was smiling, too, but his smile was his whole face, with his ears waggling at the corners of his mouth.

Ranga was invisible and enormous and hot and cold and smooth and rough and tingly and still and…

'I'm very glad that you wrote to me—you were very brave!'

…pleased and proud and, *Oh, wait until Harkishen hears about this! And Appa and Amma! And Ajji and Ajja and*….But there was no time left in life to list all the others!

Donald Bradman!!! There before him, alive, and talking to *him*.

'Come and sit with me, and tell me all about yourself.'

Sir Donald took Ranga's arm and they sat on one of the sofas.

'Which part of India do you come from?'

Ranga looked at him.

'I've been to Bombay, and Colombo—but that's

Ceylon, isn't it!'

Ranga looked at him.

'Say something, Ranga!' said Kumar, in his ear, with a hoarse voice, though not exactly like a horse. 'For India!'

'!!!'

That was where he tried, but only gulped.

'India gaagi! *For India*!'

Ranga sat up even straighter than the straightest bat known to W.G. Grace.

He gulped.

He swallowed.

He tried to undry his mouth.

'Hello, Shri Bradman!'

'I beg your pardon?'

Ranga suddenly remembered one of his lessons.

'Hello, *Mr* Bradman!'

Kumar nudged him and shout-whispered in his ear: 'Sir! *Sir*!'

'Hello Mr Bradman, sir.'

'*Speak louder, Rao*!'

'Hello, Mr Bradman sir!'

'It's "Sir!" "*Sir*!"' Ranga looked around at his teacher.

'Well, let's not worry too much about the "Sir", shall we. I've had it for a couple of years and I don't use it much. Now, you were telling me about where you come from.'

Ranga looked at Kumar, who nodded and smiled.

'Akkithimmanahalli, Sir Donald Bradman, sir. I come from Akkithimmanahalli. But that is not my middle name.'

'Ah,' said the great man, wisely.

And they were friends, one because he could easily say Akkithimmanahalli, the other because he couldn't, and it didn't matter that his batting average was 99.94, or, indeed, that Ranga didn't have one yet.

'Well, now,' said Sir Donald, after Earth had circled the entire universe three-and-a-half times. 'Captain of India: that means that you must have a team. I would like to meet them, if you will allow me to?'

How could a great man get even greater?!

'Oh, yes, Sir Bradman! I would like to allow that very much!'

'Very well, then—let's go out to bat together!'

That was how easy it was for a great man to get even greater.

Sir Donald took Ranga's hand, and neither worried about this, even though Ranga knew that he would be a man very shortly.

The pair led the way out of the Captain's cabin, the immaculately-uniformed Captain Mellonie behind them, followed by Kumar and Mr Cockle and the steward, who happened to be from Hyderabad.

'I suppose they're on the Boat Deck, playing cricket?' said *The Don*, who knew quite a bit about boys, whether they were Indian or not, so it wasn't really a question.

They walked out into the bright sunshine, the lifeboat-lined Boat Deck still damp from its early-morning wash-down, brown faces shouting at each other, even the girls—and running helter-skelter between stumps and rails and to just below the funnel.

Kumar clapped his hands.

'Everybody! Hello!' He remembered that he was not in his classroom. 'HELLO!'

Everybody stopped shouting and helter-skeltering and started wondering why Kumar was helloing at them again, which he had already done at breakfast, before everyone ate their strange Weeties with milk and lots of sugar.

'Good morning everybody!'

But they quickly lost interest in Kumar, even though they all liked him, because there was the very strange sight behind him, beside him, of Ranga holding hands with a strange man.

Kumar turned to Ranga, smiling. 'I think that you should introduce your new friend, Ranga!'

For once Ranga didn't think about Harkishen's *'let the world decide'* advice. He stepped forward, letting go of the world's greatest hand.

'This is Sir Donald Bradman.'

!?!!?!!! ?!!!!?!!!!!?!!!!!! ?!!!!!!?!!!!!!!?!!!! ?!!!?!!!!!!!!! ?!!!!!!!!!!!!,but even more so, there being so many more young Indians this time, as well as several Ten Pound Poms.

'Good morning boys! Oh! I see that I am wrong! Good morning boys and *girls*!'

Was there such a thing as greathood?!

Excitement rippled like a happy storm whispering across a cricket ocean on an especially beautiful day at the Adelaide Oval just before the coin was tossed into the warming air.

'I have met your Captain, and I know that you will do very well in Australia!'

Then he walked slowly around the team, with Ranga introducing each person in turn. *The Don* asked each one about their cricket and where they came from and told them how handsome they were, or beautiful in one or two cases.

'Right!' said Sir Don, when he'd met everyone, including Bandyopadhyay. 'Who's going to bowl to me?!'

Serious injuries were only just avoided as everybody rushed to get the ball, which had been snaffled quite unfairly by Kumar.

Whose best ball disappeared down the funnel.

Another was quickly provided by Mr Cockle, who knew why most of the Ten Pound Poms would become Australians, as well as the Dutch, who didn't know the difference between a 'roo and a rat.

Sixteen balls later—that was two overs—*The Don* handed the bat to Ranga. 'Well, boys and girls, I think it's time for me to retire, again! I have to get back to my business or I'll get the sack!'

Ranga thought that this was a very strange thing for *The Don* to say.

'I wish you all very good luck, and I hope you beat the Vics!'

Ranga had no idea what "the Vics" meant, but

thought that they might also be Australians and fitted in somewhere.

The prospect of someone beating Australia particularly pleased the Ten Pound Poms, though most of them would become Australians themselves one day, if they knew what was good for them, now that the Indians had a god on their side.

The Gasbags

Fair dinkum, Amber, if it had been an Olympic sport, Clive could have farted for Australia! He was an absolute beauty. A virtuoso. A while ago he farted the entire *William Tell Overture* with the Adelaide Symphony Orchestra. It was broadcast on the ABC–you know, one of those concerts where they have the van outside and all those black cables snaking around all over the place. At the end he was the only one in the auditorium, up there on the stage, by himself. Had to stand up, of course, for the whole performance. What stamina! Most of us watched it on telly. They cut the ABC's budget after that. Yair, really affected the ABC's bottom line.

Clive wasn't the only one in his family with talent. His grandfather Cedric, on his mother's side, so he was a Ramsbottom, not a Bottomly, emptied the Sydney Town Hall in forty-five seconds one night. He let it all out. They had pressure problems with their famous Grand Organ for some weeks after the event, and it was noted that several sections of heritage gold leaf around the walls were slightly blistered. Cedric was pushing ninety at the time, so this was a magnificent effort, and he really could not have been held account-able for the problems caused by the mass exodus on to George Street and the unseemly behaviour exhibited around taxi ranks and bus stations. He went on to become one of Australia's most famous irrigators—colonic, that is.

Cousin Cecil was another one. He was a bushy up in the Riverina. Dunno what he grew—he was always a bit vague about that—but he was a great handyman—they all were in those days—and inventor. One of his

best-known inventions was what he called the
Distressed Air Applicator Device, which he used for
pumping up tyres around the farm. Truckies driving
between Adelaide and Broken Hill and Sydney would
often drop in for a top-up—they swore that tyres filled
with Cecil's distressed air lasted longer than any, and
never got stolen. He tried to protect his intellectual
property legally, but the Patents Office doors always
seemed to be closed when he came to town. The
DAAD was pretty much like those tyre-pumping
things you use at service stations, except that it had a
nozzle at both ends and came with a jar of Vaseline.

Great-Aunt Celia was the quiet one, so to speak, in
the family, but a dormant volcano. She'd sit in the
corner of the lounge, or on the front verandah, or
once or twice a week on the back verandah, watching
the world go by and monitoring how far the cockatoos
had got ripping the paint-work off around the windows, puffing on one of those clay pipes that you can

only buy from dodgy archaeologists, occasionally leaning over for a quiet but generally harmless bit of deflation. This was the interesting thing about her aerial evacuations, that set her apart from the rest of the family—she specialised in noise, rather than aroma. Consequently she was less often alone, compared to everyone else in the family. The other distinguishing aspect of Great-Aunt Celia was that she generally spoke in Capitals and if someone pummelled her bottom she would involuntarily but with great effect punctuate her Capitalised sentences with an engaging variety of bottom burps, delighting primary school boys and some girls from a considerable radius for decades.

Cliff was Clive's second cousin, once removed, who had to be removed from his classroom more than once. Ironically, he became the family's first qualified school teacher, at Broken Hill's School of the Air. This was in the days before electrical machines, which was not a problem for him, given both his mechanical ingenuity and traditional airs and graces.

Charles, Cliff's younger brother, became a lawyer in Hobart, where he was well-known for his uncanny ability to rebut his opponents' arguments and to follow any line of reasoning to its absolute end.

Werner van Dijke was a particularly famous Dutch relative, a professional dam builder, who developed a new method for blasting low-lying soil and rocks, making them even more low-lying, with perfectly-positioned banks on either side of the excavation for use as roads and bicycle tracks. After the war he was recruited by NASA to develop new methods of rocket propulsion, unfortunately meeting a terrible and unfulfilled end when he lit his cigar in the command capsule of a Saturn V rocket as it was idling on the launch pad at Cape Canaveral, going through its final test sequences before the astronauts boarded. Probably a good thing, really, for them. And quite certainly an educational experience and powerful lesson for von Braun that he no doubt didn't come across when he was designing Germany's V2 rockets. His sister Cornelia, on the other hand, was quite undistinguished, living a quiet clog-filled life in the vicinity of Dwarsvaart.

Clive's son, Cassius, was one who rose, literally, to great heights, in the field of gliding. He actually held the world record for both heights achieved and aerial longevity, but his inherent modesty prevented him from claiming his due recognition. He would always take off and land at different airfields, often hundreds of kilometres apart. In this way no-one realised that he had achieved an amazing feat or twigged as to how he did it. It was actually quite simple, from a family point of view. If his thermal began to lose power over Benalla or wherever, he'd simply externalise his own internal combustion engine waste products and jack up a few hundred metres, and so on. Occasionally, if a tug appeared to be in trouble hauling him off the runway he'd do much the same, boosting its power. I heard several tug pilots, when they came down, telling anyone who cared to listen how they'd experienced a sudden boost of power just when they were regretting their Scrooge-like decision to not pay a life insurance premium when it fell due.

There's no doubt that Cassius could also have beaten every hot air balloon record, but, being a slightly vain man, he refused the thought of being encased in an anonymous and definitely unflattering space suit. Although he never mentioned it, being enclosed hermetically in such an environment might also have been a factor in his thinking.

Yes, Amber, you're probably thinking that Cassius was unique in our family, being able to keep his talent more or less to himself, but there was one other, Claude Windmill. Claude was a sapper at Gallipoli, usually engaged in creating tunnels under enemy lines. He became quite well known towards the end of our stay there when a stray Turkish bullet–or it could have been one of ours–flashed between his legs in the latrine, which was next to a forest of pine trees, the consequent explosion creating the famous Lone Pine.

But, while we are all thrilled with this, the reason we're so proud of him was what he did right at the end, so to speak.

As you might know, Lord Kitchener persuaded the British War Cabinet that the Gallipoli Campaign back in 1915 was a lost cause, and a mass evacuation of the ANZACs was planned for the middle of December. Deceit would be the key to success–the Turks had to believe that we were mostly all still there, even when we all were happily steaming away back to Egypt. Lots of sneaky ideas were put into play, mainly different ways to keep firing rifles towards the enemy when no-one was actually firing them. But–and this is still covered by the Official Secrets Act–Sapper Windmill volunteered to stay behind, no pun intended, and add to the confusion in his own—indeed our family's—special way.

Winter in Turkey is not like Christmas turkey—it was very cold and the mud floors of the trenches were icy and treacherous—you could skate on them. None of this fazed Claude, nor the prospect of being discovered by the Turk who, Claude imagined, would be a little annoyed, even though they couldn't speak English. He'd been stocking up on raisins and sultanas for some time, to make a Christmas pudding, which he nobly decided to forgo, in order to maximise his impact.

In this vein, Claude set out to augment the work of the various devices set in motion earlier by his comrades. He was to tell his biographer later that the first thing this entailed was the need to amplify his resources. He did this by manufacturing a passable version of the old Elizabethan collar—you know, the things vets give you to stop your dog licking the stitches out. The only downsides to this ingenious piece of apparatus were that he couldn't wear trousers and it kept knocking against the trench walls as he skated from pozzy to pozzy, slowing him down a bit. The upside was that the noise probably added to the enemy's confusion, even terror.

When he got to a firing point he'd bend over, point the collar at the Turkish trenches, turn his head upside down between his knees to get his bearings, and *rat-a-tat-tat* amplified through the collar, then run off to the next pozzy.

When daylight came he could see Anzac Cove was empty: his task was done. He took off the collar, found a pair of trousers and a great coat, found a billy and filled it with snow, and had his first hot brew for half a century. He didn't have long to wait before several giant bayonets crept around a corner and he met the Turk! He spent the next five weeks in a

Turkish prison camp further up the peninsula, at a small town called Anafartalar, would you believe!

His interrogation was intense, face to face—the Turks initially deeply suspicious, to begin with, as to why he had been left behind, but the discussions soon became quite spasmodic. Finally, with a shared air of resignation at his recalcitrance, the authorities decided that it would be better for all for him to be confined further away, quite a way away, in their only open prison, in Constantinople. But he insisted on being taken to Istanbul, because of its bovine connotations, and he subsequently and somewhat consequently spent a happy three years there.

Sir Calvin ("Kilvun") Windsor ("Wunzer") was the most distinguished member of our family. He had a most successful practice in New Zealand as a specialist gastro-endocrinologist, and fitted—genealogically— Prime Minister Keating's description of Australia being "the arse-end of the world".

All of these multi-talented folk had a common ancestor, Cecilia Lowbrow, who emigrated to Australia from England in the late 1880s and became the Chaffey brothers' cook in Mildura. She took such a liking to the resulting dried fruits–raisins and sultanas in particular, but also dates–that her DNA was terminally altered to make sub-sequent generations' jeans extremely and continually and conspicuously prone to sudden and often spectacular pop-offs relocating themselves from a strictly private place to more widely populated areas where it was often heart-wrenchingly difficult for contiguous humans to effect a timely egress. I believe that the term "lift-off" may have had its origins in Cecilia's pioneering outback efforts.

It was she who had a Family Crest designed, and Latin motto created which, translated, means, roughly, "Be Not Halfarted".

Sadly, I'm the end of the line, fighting a rear-guard action here in Kalgoorlie, nowadays your mother's bouncer and general dog's body. It'll be good to retire next year, you know, so that I can get out into the fresh air and smell the roses instead of a century of family history, not that there are many roses out here, but you know what I mean...

Oh? Yes, Amber, Mary Poppins was also one of us...

Then there was the White Russian branch of the family, the Popovs...

...and the Aztec Popocatapetls...

...and the...

Descendants

Ranga lay awake. Jemmy's bed was not like his bed at home, and he thought about all the beds he'd been in, and tried to sleep in, since they'd left India. How many was it now? There was his hard trestle bed in Akkithimmanahalli, then the luggage racks on the trains to Bombay—they were fun, but squashy. The fourth was his top bunk on H Deck, swaying and rolling as *Strathnaver* brought them to Australia. Fifth was at the hallowed MCG, where he couldn't sleep. And now here at Jemmy's farm.

Jemmy's place was away from Niamong—it was called Quimbilong, which was much harder to say than Akkithimmanahalli. When Mr Brister turned his ute into the long driveway from the dusty road the stars were diamonding the sky and a young boy's eyelids were becoming quite difficult to keep apart, even though they belonged to the Captain of India.

The first night at Quimbilong felt like being back home—monkeys ran backwards and forwards all over the sleepout's roof. He hadn't known that there were monkeys in Australia, or that they were just as much a nuisance here as in India. The funny thing, though, was that he hadn't seen any monkeys anywhere so far, except for Ruchika. Maybe Australian monkeys only came out at night.

'Come on, Ranga—breakfast! Sun's up!'

Ranga smiled. He already liked Mrs Brister—*Shrimati* Brister—and thought that he'd never seen anyone bustle so much. 'I heard monkeys on the roof last night.'

'Monkeys?' she laughed. 'I think the only monkeys around here are people who wear shorts and eat all my food!'

'G'day, Ranga,' said Jemmy, 'want to feed the chooks after breakfast?'

The sun was well up and feeling like the middle of the dry season. Jemmy showed Ranga how to mix up the bran and pollard and potato peelings, and stir everything into a nice sticky mess.

'This'll turn into some pretty good eggs.'

Ranga looked at him, wondering whether Jemmy might have been out in the sun too long.

'We'll come back tonight and collect them.'

The day in front of them, Ranga thought, might be better than he'd thought, because the last thing that had happened at the school the day before was that Mr Olney had declared, on behalf of the Education Department, but no-one knew why, tomorrow, which was today, a School Holiday.

'Come over and meet Old Mary.'

He led Ranga around behind the barn. An elephant! Oops! Not quite! A giant horse!!

'Meet Old Mary.'

Ranga looked up, and up. She must have been like Uthaishravastu, the horse which Devendra, the Lord of the Angels, rode into battle against the forces of evil. It was almost like standing on the wharf at Bombay, looking at the *Strathnaver*.

'We're going out on her today–I'll show you the farm. Then I'll take you into Mr Cross's–he told Miss Hendley that he'd take you out with him on his run today.'

Ranga wasn't sure about this. He'd seen Mr Cross at the railway station, and heard him welcome the team, so he must have been an important person.

Perhaps he was Niamong's Patel? And what was Mr Cross's "run"?

And *wh*en were they going to play the cricket match?

Mr Cross walked across the yard from the general store, which he owned, nodding at Scratcher's father as he slid open the large doors of the grain store.

'How is it, Bert?'

Scratcher's Dad only grunted, because he knew that Mr Cross wasn't listening.

'That Indian kid's going to be pretty impressed.'

Mr Cross walked over to a long box perched on two trestles. He walked around it one way, then around it the other way, admiring it. He bent over it and polished the top with his sleeve, seeing the reflection of the doorway in the gleaming wood.

'Isn't it a beaudy!' Mr Cross polished the box again, looking at his reflection in the wood. 'Let's get this into the hearse.'

The men lifted the coffin carefully and laid it in the back of the vehicle, closing the door after it.

'See ya later, Bert, gotta get on with it, and pick up the Indian.'

He started the engine and in a few minutes was dusting down the road, the dust respectfully following in slow motion.

On either side of the road, wherever a bit of water had lain after the last rain, a rabbit or two was nibbling the grass, or excavating a burrow, dropping a pellet or two when the strain got too much.

Past the station, past the silo with its flocking pigeons. 'Ah, there they are.'

He stopped the other side of the level crossing, beside Old Mary, the hearse engine purring like a cat that still had all of its nine lives in front of it, as long as a train wasn't coming behind it, and it wasn't using the vehicle for its intended purpose.

'G'day, boys!'

'G'day, Mr Cross. This is Ranga,' said Jemmy.

Mr Cross looked at the Captain of India.

'Good morning, Mr Cross. Thank you for taking me for a ride in your vehicle.'

'No worries, young fella. Hop down and we'll get going…can't leave our…er…customers waiting!'

Jemmy held Ranga's arm while he slid off Old Mary's back. ' See ya later, Ranga! I'll bring Old Mary up to the cemetery to pick you up.'

'In ya go, young fella, and be careful the box doesn't dazzle you in the sun!'

Ranga looked at the long, gleaming box in the back,

and wondered. And his hairs prickled as he wondered why Jemmy would pick him up at the cemetery.

'Doesn't go too fast, on these roads. And we have to show a bit of respect,' said Mr Cross, without looking at him, even though he was going so slowly.

The hearse slowed down even more after a few minutes, if that was possible, and turned off into a farm drive. Mr Cross was humming his favourite funeral song. 'Open the gate, young fella, and make sure to close it after I've gone through it. Don't worry about the dead sheep. Lots of bunnies today!'

The hearse pulled up outside an old house. Dr Pendle came out as Mr Cross killed the engine (not that he was looking for any more business) and climb-ed out.

'Good morning, Mr Cross. Ah, I see you've brought the Captain of India! She's in the front room.'

'I thought she would be. They always are.'

Mr Cross walked around to the back of the hearse.

'Give me a hand, will you, doc. You, too, Ranga.'

It was Ranga's first turn with a coffin, and he scraped his knuckles under the box as they pulled it across the hearse's floor.

'Get the door, Ranga. Yes, keep it open—we won't be a minute.'

The men carried the coffin into the house, Dr Pendle tucking his stethoscope back into a pocket. Up on the hill the rabbits did a little multiplying, then the men came out, this time with quite a bit of grunting and careful stumbling.

'That's it. Slip her in.'

She was slipped into the hearse and the door closed down behind her.

'Oh, I nearly forgot,' said Dr Pendle, 'just before you arrived they rang and said could you drop over to Nhillum before you went back.'

Mr Cross, back in his funereal chariot, looked at his watch and nodded. 'Should be able to make it. Hop in, Ranga.'

Ranga hopped in, but this time he didn't look back at the box—it would just have to gleam in the sun by itself.

They drove back down the track to the gate, a rabbit scooting across the road in front of them, just missing by a whisker joining whoever it was in the coffin.

The hearse turned back onto the Nhillum road, bump-ing past Quimbilong, where Old Mary and Jemmy and Ranga had been earlier in the morning, and stuff that was going to turn into eggs. The dust cloud-ed over them as the hearse smoothed past, Ranga's arm waving out of the window at Mrs Brister, just in case she was looking.

Mr Cross and his quiet and very quiet indeed passengers pulled up outside a run-down building in Nhillum, the home of Niamong's bitter enemies. A faded sign 'Undertakers to the Cockies' peeled over the front of the shed. He opened the back of the hearse and went into the building, waving to Ranga to stay in the hearse.

'*Two*?!' exclaimed Mr Cross, when he saw what was in the hot shed.

'I'm sorry, Mr Cross. The other one was, um, a little unexpected. But they're going to do her in Niamong this afternoon.'

Most Nhillumites always said they wouldn't be seen dead in Niamong, but Nhillum didn't have a cemetery and Niamong did, so Niamong always had the last laugh, even when they weren't laughing.

'Well, if they've both gotta go they've both gotta

go!' grunted Mr Cross, thinking that two last laughs were better than none.

'Or in this case, Mr Cross, they both gotta went!'

'Get the other end.' Mr Cross was not amused by anything said in Nhillum.

'Righto, Mr Cross. And, as they say in the trade, no coughin' in the coffin.'

Or anything said by a Nhillumite.

They lifted the first coffin, took it outside and put it into the hearse, the warm sun smiling down on them, as it had no idea what was going on.

The second one was a good deal heavier, resulting in much grunting and heaving, and a little almost-dropping. Unfortunately when they got it to the hearse they discovered that it wouldn't quite fit, either beside or on top of the other two. They put it down, one end on the road, the other on the tailgate, while they looked at the problem for a bit.

'Yep,' Mr Cross said, after quite a bit of looking, 'on top,' and then they were on their way back to Nia-mong, dusting down the road again, the third coffin strapped to the roof.

Ranga looked straight ahead, all the way to Niamong.

Bells were ringing from the towers of each of Nia-mong's churches, one after the other, slowly.

Main Street was deserted, with shopkeepers locking their doors and walking away, heading towards the edge of town and the old cemetery. It hadn't been used for quite a while, probably because of the war, and several families of rabbits had decided that it could be made to quite good use.

People were walking into the cemetery, black blotches in their best Sunday clothes, even though it was Thursday.

Gravestones stood at various angles beside several paths, some just about quite fallen over, others with dried flowers standing crookedly in cracked jars. At an open patch, loosely dotted with rabbits, was a freshly-dug grave, with *another* freshly-dug grave almost touching it. And another!! The first and second were empty, and Gravyhead was climbing out of the third, using a spade to help him get out of the hole.

By this time Mr Cross was gunning the hearse towards Niamong, peering around the ropes holding the third coffin on the roof. There wasn't time to drive respectfully slowly. They finally squealed around the last corner and halted rapidly in front of the church, unfortunately with the top coffin sliding off the roof and onto the bonnet.

Ranga's eyelids were blinking furiously at the front coffin, which was just above his nose, and the back coffins which were pressing him against the windscreen, hoping that the windscreen wipers didn't get going. Mr Cross climbed out, taking in the scene, and then looked for the pall bearers.

They weren't there, which, understandably, appalled him. However, Mrs Phelpps rushed up, which may or may not have been a relief to him.

'MR CROSS! THANK GOD YOU'VE ARRIVED! EVERYBODY'S HERE, INCLUDING THE INDIANS–HELLO RANGA! BUT WHERE ARE THE REVERENDS?!'

'They're not here?? What day is it?!'

'WHAT DAY? IT'S THURSDAY. WE ALWAYS HAVE OUR FUNERALS ON A THURSDAY. WASHING DAY MONDAY, FISH ON...'

'The fourth Thursday?'

Mrs Phelpps checked her mental calendar, arriving at the correct answer, suddenly realising what this meant. She watched as Mr Cross swivelled quickly and leapt back into the hearse, climbing across Ranga from the passenger side door. 'Gotta problem, Ranga!' He gunned the motor, pressed the accelerator to the floor, forgot Ranga completely, who was trying to peer a-round the slightly dislodged front coffin, and sped down the hill towards the *Lalor's Arms*.

At the graveside, or sides, people were doing what any-one would do in the circumstances: they looked at their watches, the sky, each other, into the empty graves. There was even the beginning of a rivering flow from grave to empty grave, and a little bit of standing on little bits left by the rabbits.

'Rabbits are bad this year,' said Jemmy's father.

'Good for the hatters, though,' said his neighbour from two miles down the road.

Sahaj looked at Ruchika and Subhashini and the rest of his team mates, and then at the vanishing Ranga, wondering if Australia had suddenly gone mad.

Mr Cross and Ranga and the hearse and the three coffins pulled up outside the pub, sounds of singing floating out as Niamong's undertaker got out of his vehicle. He flicked a look skywards, which resulted in no assistance whatsoever–there was never a god a-round when you needed one. He walked inside, Ranga sparing one eye to see where he went.

The singing stopped for a few seconds, then began again, moving from the back of the hotel towards the front, other men raucously joining in the chorus, with much goodwill all round, Reverend Greensleeves staggering a little and the good Father Michael trying unsuccessfully to convert a couple of Protestants on the way, with everyone asking him whether the Pope was a Catholic.

Mr Cross tumbled the clergymen into his vehicle, which pretty well shut them all up, with six of them on the one seat, and none being able to breathe. Ranga tried to think what advice Harkishen Singh would give him in this situation, but could only think of Brigadier Hill in the shower.

At the church lych-gate Mrs Phelpps had gathered a fine body of men and boys, ready for the return of the coffins. She thought that she'd better get them organised, for when Mr Cross got back.

'Now! THREE STRAIGHT LINES! NO! *SIX* STRAIGHT LINES! SIX LINES! NOT ONE LINE OF SIX! THAT'S RIGHT. THREE IN EACH LINE. THREE IN EACH LINE! I SAID THREE IN EACH LINE! YES, THAT'S RIGHT! NO, NOT LIKE THAT! YOU! YES, YOU! YES, YOU'RE GOING TO BE PALL BEARERS! NO, THAT'S NOTHING TO DO WITH NEPAL! YES. NO. YES. NOW FACE THIS WAY. THIS WAY! YES, THAT'S RIGHT. NOW STAND STILL. STILL! Ah, here comes Mr Cross!'

The hearse creamed down the road, squealing to a halt, the front coffin finally giving up its struggle and sliding to the ground with a thump, after bouncing all over the bonnet. Mr Cross opened the doors.

The clerics were all very happy, until they saw Mrs Phelpps.

'GOOD AFTERNOON, REVERENDS. SO NICE OF YOU TO COME.[6] RIGHT, MEN, YOU KNOW WHAT TO DO.'

Her pall party of men and boys quickly broke ranks, and probably wind. Some rushed to the fallen coffin, the others hurried to the back of the hearse.

'HURRY UP! HURRY UP!'

Well, what a thing to say.

'YES, YES, THAT'S RIGHT! NOW, UP ON THE SHOULDERS! GET THEM UP! GET THEM UP!'

---

[6] We're not sure whether this is an example of irony or facetiousness, or plain sarcasm. Knowing Mrs Phelpps, it was probably all three. *Editor.*

They did, but unfortunately they mixed up their lines and the coffins ended up at all sorts of angles and across the three groups.

'COME ON! COME ON! YOU GO OVER THERE! YOU COME HERE. NO, NOT THE INDIANS! *YOU* GIVE HIM THAT ONE AND HE CAN TAKE THIS ONE. NOT THAT ONE! *THAT* ONE! YES, THAT ONE. YES, YES. YES. RIGHT, REVERENDS! *REVERENDS*!! LEAD THE WAY!'

The clerics stumbled through the flotilla to the front, where they assembled side by side, straightening out their clothes and calming their beating hearts. Ranga decided that he should follow, rather than lead, just this once. After all, these were all Australians, not Indians. His friends gathered with him, Bandyopadhyay and Kumar tagging along behind, completely mystified.

Mrs Phelpps battleshipped to the front and looked at her navy, tossing about in a rather choppy swell.

'VERY GOOD! OFF WE GO! COME ALONG, FATHER MICHAEL! STOP HANGING BACK THERE!'

'But I haven't got one today, Mrs Phelpps!'

'NEVER MIND ABOUT THAT, FATHER— YOU'RE HERE SO YOU MAY AS WELL FALL IN WITH THE REST! MAKE ROOM THERE!'

Wisely he joined the third coffin party.

Everyone set off. From the side they looked like a centipede, or was it a millipede. I suppose it depends on whether you like hundreds or thousands...

Mrs Phelpps was now quite a bit out front, so to speak, as she looked back.

'COME ON! COME ON! BUCK IT UP! THAT'S IT! COME ON! KEEP IT UP! WATCH IT! YOU! DON'T DROP IT! GOOD. GOOD.

NEARLY THERE. NOT TOO FAST! *NOT TOO FAST!* **I SAID NOT TOO FAST!**'

All this shouting was frightening the rabbits. Everybody at the graves turned around to look at the galloping pall bearers, Mrs Phelpps band-majoring the troop at a very quick quick march, coffins rushing down the hill towards their doom.

The three columns split and juggernaughted to the three adjacent graves, with much heaving and puffing, and adjusting of best hats and pocket watch chains. They lowered, without the dignity the occupants were surely entitled to expect, the three coffins. The clerics took up their stations, Greensleeves at the middle grave, the lesser Protestants on either side, but none of them sure that they were with their correct late parishioners. Father Michael remained at the back, wondering if there was anyone there who could be persuaded to switch sides. And Ranga just wondered.

'Dearly beloved, we are gathered here today in the sight of God...,' began the Reverend Greensleeves, gathering dignity with his cassock.

Mrs Phelpps cleared her throat as everyone looked at him, a slight hiccup escaping his slightly dry lips as he realised that he was, in fact, at a burial, rather than a wedding.

' ...I beg your pardon...'

By this time the other ministers had got stuck into their own services, finally reaching the end at exactly the same time and together:

'...and so we commit our dear brother or sister as the case may be...'

They all paused as the pallbearers took up the straps to lower the coffins into the other world, which was really only a bit lower than this world.

And as each cleric suddenly became wide-eyed and sober. And all the pallbearers, who were mostly sober to begin with, became wide-eyed and puzzled.

And they all slowly disappeared, the three coffins and their eighteen lowerers sliding gracefully downwards and out of sight, the sides of the graves looking like Swiss cheese, certainly holier than thou.

Scores of rabbits tumbled out of their holes and tunnels in the various graves and mêléed with the sinking mourners…

…as the clerics, like brandied marionettes, followed them into the underworld, slowly and jerkily and magnificently followed by the rest of the crowd, Ranga included and definitely now thinking of innings, and the rest of his team, and Bandyopadhyay and Kumar, as well as Mr Braden (I'm pleased to say) and Mrs Phelpps and even Miss Hendley, as the whole area around the graves collapsed, women shrieking and men cursing and everyone scrabbling in the clay and rocks and dust and rabbits and coffins and straps and reverends and friends and enemies and probably one or two ghosts, trying to save themselves.

Wait until Appa and Amma and Ajji and Ajja and the other Ajji and Ajja hear about this! And all my aunts and uncles and cousins! thought Ranga, tangling with people he'd never met, at the very bottom of the gravest part of the graveyard, looking up at the bright blue sky.

And Jemmy outside the cemetery fence, laughing atop an animal that would still have been seen even if it, too, had slid into the bowels of the earth, or wherever it was that angels feared to tread, unless they were well padded up.

Twins in Dock

Burton Bekker, Court Reporter

Melbourne, Friday

Comedic twins Bob, aged 37:7:3:2:14:37:02, and Ben, aged 37:7:3:2:15:00:11, Merriman, known professionally as *The Merrymans*, appeared in the Melbourne Magistrates Court (est. 1858) on a charge of affray yesterday at 10am Eastern Summer Time.

The case, before Assistant Deputy Chief Magistrate Penny Courtcastle, 49, began in some confusion, due to the fact that Deputy Chief Magistrate Cecil Charger,

53, had reportedly become suddenly indisposed, due to having breakfasted on a smoked kipper prepared by his wife Cecilia, 52, the best-by-date being slightly obscured and a considerable time in the past, and her being temporarily without her reading glasses, resulting in Assistant Deputy Chief Magistrate Penny Courtcastle, 49, having to cut short her morning session with her personal trainer and hurry to the court, to fill-in for the apparently indisposed Deputy Chief Magistrate Cecil Charger, 53.

Senior Constable Ross Househusband, 31 and probably a bit, taking the oath in the witness box, said that he received a radio message whilst on patrol with his relatively new partner, Probationary Constable Jaqueline Oneoff (44), to attend a fracas at 1,939 Capes Street, Briar Valley.

'The radio was a bit crackly, Your Worship, causing me to have doubts about the event that we had to deal with. I had not come across the word 'fracas' before, and am certain that it was not mentioned at the Academy, although other words that sounded something like 'fracas' *were* used, quite often, especially at the end of the day.'

Senior Constable Househusband, 31 and probably a bit, referred to his notebook.

'I switched off the radio and began to discuss the word that caused me a problem with my partner Probationary Constable Jaqueline Oneoff (44).'

At this stage the Bench interposed a question.

'Senior Constable Househusband, 31 and probably a bit, are any problems that you may have been having with Probationary Constable Oneoff (44) pertinent, or indeed relevant, to the case before me?'

Senior Constable Househusband, 31 and probably a bit, apologised to the Bench and made it clear that the problem that he was referring to was not Probationary Constable Oneoff (44), with whom he had a very good working relationship but not one that he thought should interest the Bench, but rather that he referred to the word 'fracas', or whatever word it was that the operator (age unknown) at Base had used.

Senior Constable Househusband, 31 and probably a bit, again referred to his notes.

'After discussing the matter with Probationary Constable Oneoff (44) we were left, as Your Worship would appreciate, with no option other than to proceed to 1,939 Capes Street, Briar Valley, and leave the clarification of the offending word until our return to Base.

'On arrival at 1,939 Capes Street, Briar Valley we discovered the accused wrestling on the grass verge beside the road, causing my partner Probationary Constable Oneoff (44) to snigger something about virgins, which, as a Senior Constable, and in mixed company, I considered inappropriate, though not without a degree of humour, in view of the un-disputed fact that such people are rarely encountered in my job.'

At this point there came a spirited "Boom boom" from the dock, drawing a stern stare from Deputy Chief Magistrate Penny Courtcastle, 49, who was likely thinking about her personal trainer and wished to see the case proceeded with with a degree of expeditious-ness.

'That is very interesting, officer, but I have other things on my mind, and things to do which include, if you recall, this case.'

Obviously quite unused to facetiousness, if not actual sarcasm, Senior Constable Househusband, 31 and probably a bit, again referred to his notes.

'If the Bench pleases, Your Worship. On arrival at 1,939 Capes Street, Briar Valley, as read out earlier, my partner Probationary Constable Oneoff (44) and my-self discovered the accused wrestling on the grass verge beside the road. We both together and in unison descended from our bi-cycles and called out to the deceased, um, the accused, to cease their activity and desist from re-engaging in same, until Probationary Constable Oneoff (44) and I could effect appropriate identification of the potentially alleged offenders, that is, them.'

At this point he fixed his gaze on the dock, and all in the body of the court turned to stare at the pair who were, by this stage, undoubtedly alleged offenders, otherwise why would they be there, the Dock not being a stage?

'And...?' Deputy Chief Magistrate Penny Courtcastle, 49, cleverly brought him back to the business in hand.

'Your Worship. Constable Oneoff (44) and I then managed to separate the pair of gentlemen who we would later allege to be the offenders, and proceeded to question them, beginning with attempting to ascertain their identities by asking them their names.

'My partner, forty-four-year-old Probationary Constable Oneoff, and myself had considerable difficulty at this point, as the pair of potentially alleged offenders was or were, whilst now vertical, still locked together in what my partner Probationary Constable Oneoff (44) and I determined was not a friendly embrace, and which was accompanied by much shouting of words to the effect that the other potential alleged offender was a liar, although, to my embarrassment, as you might understand Your Worship, their mutual means of expression was more extensive and carried nuances that were not within the sub-category of subtle.'

Deputy Chief Magistrate Penny Courtcastle, 49, again interrupted at this point, clearly having given up on thoughts of her personal trainer, but cogniscant of the march of time towards the possibility of Danish open sandwiches with smoked salmon and avocado, and perhaps a small glass of chardonnay.

'Senior Constable—I don't know your age—we are here to try some alleged offenders, not the Bench!'

Again there was a "Boom boom" from the dock, followed from the same source, or nearly so, by what sounded to this reporter like the word 'liar', one or both of which brought a stern rebuke from the Bench that if this occurred again one or both of the perpetrators, depending on court officers' ability to properly identify same, would be removed immediately to the cells below and made to miss their lunch. This being Vegemite sandwiches and bananas caused those in the dock, including a Police Officer (who was not an offender although he was known to favour conducting regular and not-infrequent security checks of a certain well-known local hamburger establishment), to straighten up and pay both attention and respect.

'Yes, Your Worship. My partner Probationary Constable Oneoff (44) and I, demonstrating how well we worked together, managed to separate the persons who we could now see were potential alleged offenders, and then we discovered that these persons were, in fact, identical.'

'Thank you, Senior Constable—I don't know your age—I can see that myself.' To emphasise her ability with regard to this matter she cast her gaze at the Dock, whose inhabitants were, at that point, oblivious of her gaze or the importance of the gazer to their immediate future, being engaged in an obviously mutually-fruitless discussion about Vegemite.

'Well, Your Worship, it was at this point that I attempted to contact CIB, as this appeared to require special expertise but, unfortunately, on appraising them of the situation on the ground, I was advised that all members were unavailable due to a lack of serviceable bicycles and, in any case, no-one would be available till after lunch, at the earliest. Being thrown back on our own resources, Probationary Constable Oneoff (44) and I chose to take this as our challenge for the day and proceeded with our enquiries. To expedite matters for the Court, Your Worship, we engaged in a short confabulation and decided that it would be prudent to charge the potential alleged offenders imm-ediately on the basis that this would, at one stroke, transmute them from potential *alleged* offenders to *actual* alleged offenders *and* cause them to cease using the word 'liar', which we deemed would be beneficial, there being several precedents that came to our minds.'

He took a sip of water and turned the page of his note-book.

'At this point the alleged offenders...'he looked over at the dock 'transferred their name-calling from each other to ourselves, a situation which neither Probat-ionary Constable Oneoff (44) nor I considered appro-priate, given the dignity of our profession and the fact that we represented the wider law-abiding community and were acting on their behalf, so we 'cuffed them.'

A loud cry of pain emitted from the dock, followed by another 'Boom boom', followed by a deathly silence throughout the court as everyone present realised the tragic luncheon consequences of this outburst.

'You were warned, prisoners! But you will remain in court for the time being, until you're both found guilty!' interposed Senior Constable Ross House-husband, 31 and probably a bit.

'That's enough, Senior Constable—I don't know your age—that is for *me* to say!' barked Assistant Deputy Chief Magistrate Penny Courtcastle, 49, standing quickly on her dignity and pointing a quivering finger at someone.

'Your Worship—I apologise profoundly, and would also do so profusely if it were not so close *to lunch*,' said Senior Constable Househusband, 31 and probably a bit more by this stage, looking mockingly at the dock, but not catching the alleged offenders' eyes, these being understandably averted downwards and in one case obscured by a red and orange handkerchief, which the embarrassed constable quickly returned to his jacket's breast pocket, a flamboyant gesture not without a degree of pathos.

Assistant Deputy Chief Magistrate Penny Courtcastle, 49, regaining her regal legal composure, resumed her seat—or bench—and briefly acknowledged the apology, waving perhaps a tad wearily for the case for the prosecution to continue and somewhat mollified by the dual realisation that there was no defence lawyer in court and that there would now be a couple of spare sandwiches.

'Having 'cuffed them...' Househusband (31+) looked expectantly but fruitlessly at the dock, there being some boundaries few people would consider crossing twice, '...it became apparent to both Probationary Constable Oneoff (44) and myself that the alleged offenders should be removed to the Station and processed there, it at that point beginning to rain, an event quite unexpected, in Melbourne, due to the drought. However, it being then remembered that the Station was located some twenty kilometres, or twelve miles (approximately), distant from 1,939 Capes Street, Briar Valley, but neither of us nor, indeed, the alleged offenders being critical of the Government's police-station-location-decision-criteria, the issue of removal from Place A (being 1,939 Capes Street, Briar Valley) to Place B (the Station) assumed a degree of importance not normally experienced in our line of employment, namely that there was transport available, *prima facie*, for only two, that is Probationary Constable One-off (44) and myself.

'At this point, when our dilemma became apparent to the alleged offenders, *aka* the accused, one or both of them suggested that it was all a storm in a teacup and that, all things considered, especially the weather, they should be released.

'This so enraged Probationary Constable Oneoff (44) that she lost all control of herself, so to speak, and 'cuffed the alleged offenders together. Being by this stage quite bemused by the fact that Probationary Constable Oneoff (44) had in her possession a *second* pair of handcuffs, contrary to normal practice but, in my then opinion, commendable given the circumstances as they had transpired and would no doubt continue to do so, I turned my attention to the journey to the Station and its means of effectation.'

Several coughs emanated from the bench, if not The Bench, accompanied by a rustle which could only have been from the turning pages of a pocket dictionary.

'Taking stock, I decided that I must use the resources at hand, namely our police-issue bicycles, even if discomfort was to ensue. "Get on the bikes!" I ordered severely, specifically addressed to the alleged offenders, but also to Probationary Constable Oneoff (44), who sometimes requires guidance.'

Your reporter, it must be confessed, at this stage stopped thinking of her editor (59) in strictly negative terms, perceiving, *albeit* dimly, the possibility of at least some rewards, if not accolades, from a career in court reporting, and set about (mentally) re-working this report's initial wording into the format that readers are currently reading.

'It immediately became apparent that there was a second problem,' read Senior Constable House-husband, whom your reporter saw as now being ageless, from his notes. 'Whilst my bike, er bicycle, was standard police issue, that of Probationary Constable Oneoff (44), though also of standard police issue, was of a standard developed for the use of females, which, I at first thought, precluded the transportation strategy I had in mind, namely dinking.

'However, having completed both Resourcefulness 1 and Resourcefulness 2 at the Academy in my initial training, which had also been completed by Probationary Constable Oneoff (44) but not at the same time, I instructed one of the offenders—I'm not sure which one—to sit on my cross bar, and the other, of whose exact identity I was equally unsure but did not consider germane at the time, to stand on the pedals of Probationary Constable Oneoff's bicycle whilst she sat on her saddle, legs ah akimbo.

'The defendants, at this point, made various comments about bars and pedals and pushers and passengers, and the injustice of unconvicted if not actually exemplary citizens being forced to deliver themselves to a place of incar ceration. I failed to note in my notes any of these un-pertinent comments, being particularly annoyed, with the rain enveloping us all, by their use of 'in car' and my lack of knowledge of the meaning of 'ceration'.'

Your reporter, observing that this latter was delivered in all seriousness, dropped her pencil and all thought of lunch.

'We mounted our bicycles and left 1,939 Capes Street, Briar Valley, with no regrets, and no understanding of the trials facing us between that address and the Station, which, to please the Court, included two creeks somewhat in flood, a bunch of urchins with nothing better to do, and what was later identified in the mortuary as a southern hairy-nosed wombat and described by the Coroner (51) as a 'pretty big bugger, isn't he'.

'Nevertheless, the Royal Canadian Mounted Police not having everything on their own, and as you can see, we made it back to the Station, where we parked our bicycles next to a dozen or so other bicycles, which must have just then been returned by the CIB.

'We then proceeded, Probationary Constable Oneoff (44) and myself, to book the defendants in and wring out our uniforms, which by this time and due in no small part to urchin-action—yes Your Worship, I noted the hyphen in my notes—were no longer of parade ground quality.

'At this point the point that had been causing me increasing concern from the moment of our arrival at 1,939 Capes Street, Briar Valley commenced to be shared by others, in particular at that point by Senior Sergeant Nathan Stripelick, my fifty-four-year-old senior sergeant and annual performance assessor, when, in response to my presentation of the defend-ants, asked the not-impertinent question as to which was which.'

For the third time there was a 'Boom boom' from the dock, which merely elicited a brief but somehow pity-ing glance in that direction from less than thirty-six per cent of those present.

'Well, Senior Constable,' the Bench observed, 'and what did you reply?' Your reporter noted that there was no comment made regarding ages, filing this surprise for future investigation.

'Your Worship, after consulting my detailed notes of our initial interrogation at the scene, which unfortunately suffered some urchin-related damage, compounded by the introduction of a degree of dampness from one of the two creeks and most of the clouds under which we pedalled back to the station, I am able to say that each accused the other of starting it, and each accused the other of being a veteran liar and not to be trusted with the oldest joke in the book, which, by the way, is not funny, referring as it does to a certain profession and its connection, so to speak, with my own.'

'Yes, yes,' the Bench interpolated, 'but which was which?! Indeed, *which* **is** which!'

'Um. They are, um Bob and er Ben, or Ben..and...Bob... Merriman, Your Worship.'

'**Which is which**, officer?' shouted Assistant Deputy Chief Magistrate Penny Courtcastle, 49, delivered with, your reporter thought, some menace.

The Marrymans suddenly stood up in the dock, together at once, and began shouting at each other and the Court:

'He's Bob!...He's Ben!...No, *he*'s Ben!...Liar! *I*'m Ben and *you're* Bob!...Liar yourself! You don't know *who* you are!...*You're* a joke!...*You* can't tell a joke from a jack!...I can so, *liar*!...You don't even know there should be an apostrophe in our stage name!...Do so! *You* don't know the plural of man!...Do so!...Do not!...'

'**Vegemite!**' thundered the Bench. 'Case dismissed!'

And she reached for her cell phone.

'Is that Charles Sampson, my personal trainer? Aged 29.'

The Author

Ian Burns is the fourth generation of writers in his family, his grandfather **Bernard Capes** (nephew of sometime author John Capes and brother of prolific author Harriet Capes), having nearly forty novels and anthologies published, whilst his uncle Renalt Capes had two biographies and a novel published and a screenplay produced. Ian's writing began in secondary school, extending into comedy sketches and lyrics for the stage.

The catalyst for fiction writing was a story a colleague told him about a bunch of kids riding home on the back of a huge horse, which insisted on walking through a dam! This led to his first book, Scratcher (1987).

Ian has many years' experience in education, project development and management, media concepts and production, and business and creative writing.

Ian is active in his local community, receiving a Community Australia Day Award in 2006.

He lives in Melbourne, Australia, and has three adult children and nine grandchildren.

Titles by Ian Burns

For Adults and Young Adults

The Alone Man   ISBN 978-0-9806429-6-4

The Alone Man draws on the concept of Aboriginal 'dreamtime'. It is a 'double love story' about a man's love for his wife and family and his love of the land and nature.

Set in outback Australia around 100 years ago, the story is of a simple man in a simpler time creating a micro-world as many pioneers did. He carves a farm out of the bush, courts and weds a girl from even farther out back, and raises a family.

Although he doesn't realise it, his life is a kind of poetry, with the beauty of love, of nature, and of sorrow as the themes. The book affirms all of these, and the continuity of life.

A 'prose poem' which is poetic about something as ordinary (or common) as building a life—marriage, birth, death, livelihood. The style is gentle and poetic, and the story is, at the same time, humorous and sad, touching and poignant, affirming and happy, dreamy and warm.

The Alone Man is a simple story full of understated insights that will have deep emotional resonance with readers—male and female, old and young—all over the world.

Thomas Bulford's English Companion ISBN 978-09806429-5-7

An extraordinary book, giving seminal insights into such diverse matters as Amazons and aardvarks, and the mythical or legendary Eve (of Eden), Helen (of Troy), and Joan (of Arc).

Of great importance is the book's twenty-seven categories, each with a short essay purportedly by the author, introducing each section.

Saying anything else, at this stage, would be entirely superfluous, and probably an insult.

Thomas Bulford's Essays on Life, Language & Love ISBN 978-0-9806429-0-2

Readers may be aware that Thomas Bulford died recently (though not as recently as before), and that I had what I then regarded as the onerous honour of editing his lexicographical work.

Following this, his son–Thomas Bulford Junior II–presented the Publisher (whom even I now acknowledge the need to capitalise) with a box of scribblings that he said were his 'distinguished'

father's.

On being shown these, my impression was that they were, indeed Thomas Bulford's (the senior, that is), for two reasons, though not without reservation (as some of them do appear to be at least a little out of character with the bulk of the *opus*).

Firstly, they bore a striking resemblance to the 'essays' that the Publisher insisted on being incorporated in the *English Companion* as introductions to the various definitional categories.

Secondly, and I say this with as much grace as I can, they, whilst being somewhat idiosyncratic in construction and questionable in logic, contained a number of insights into the human condition that were also occasionally present in the earlier volume.

Accordingly, with less reluctance than before, I agreed to edit this material, and offer it to readers for their judgement. *Editor*

Ranga Plays Australia ISBN 978-0-646-49692-4

It's only four years after the end of World War 2, during which there were no great cricket matches. But now things are getting back to normal: the Australians have thrashed the Poms in England (which is always, and will always be, a good thing), India has played its first Test series in Australia, and 'the Don' has retired.

In a small Bangalore village young Ranganathan Rao is musing about life in general and cricket in particular. Ranga's spinning fingers begin to itch.

Kumar, Ranga's English/Geography/History teacher introduces his pupils to an especially strange word–that he heard an Australian say during the war–and invites them to try to pronounce it and identify its meaning. After many unsuccessful attempts Kumar reveals both the word's pronunciation and meaning, and suggests that everyone might remember this, as one day they might go to Australia.

This starts Ranga thinking.

The fourth *Niamong* book.

Video

The Wisdom of Harkishen Singh   ISBN 978-1-5056409-7-7

A compilation of sayings–sometimes wise, sometimes inscrutable, sometimes humorous–of an Indian guru in post-WW2 India, as spoken to and recalled by his young protégé.

Video

<u>Beethoven!–a play with music</u>   978-0-9945976-3-2

Beethoven!
a play with music

Beethoven! is the story of a man's pursuit of music, as he struggles against increasing deafness and other periodic ailments. Whilst he is a naturally gregarious person, and loves keenly a number of ladies (even leading to proposals of marriage), his hearing problem makes him more and more isolated. Compounding this is his lack of money sense, and a sometimes-too-quick temper–which causes him to fall out with his friends and run through a string of servants. Fortunately his friends are extremely loyal on the whole, and stick with him, doing their best to help him where and when they can.

Messing With Your Mind   ISBN 978-0-9945976-5-6

How are you with cognitive dissonance? Can you carry two contradictory thoughts in your mind at the same time and still tie your shoelaces? What about three, four, five, six...? Is that shoelaces or thoughts?

Where a lot of people get into desperate trouble.

Or do they?

Murders, but are they really murders? A Dutch woman blows up her husband and then becomes best friends with an Australian Aboriginal lesbian warrior?

A Chinese grandmother seduced, not unwillingly, by a Scottish rubber planter in Malaya? Was she, in fact, a grandmother? What about their granddaughter?

Why shouldn't you start a paragraph with "the"? Can there be beauty in nonsense or desperation, farce or high drama?

What would *you* do for $20 million? $60 million? Does doing something good justify doing something bad?

Can you work it out? Is there a plot or is it a plot? Is it *possible* to work it out?

More about Twiggy and Mac...

<u>For children</u>

Scratcher ISBN 0-85561-101-4   **Ages 8-14**

Have you ever wondered why clocks have hours, and minutes, and seconds...but not firsts?
You won't find the answer to this question in this book, but Scratcher will tell you what happens if your dog goes wild in a butcher's shop,
or if an eel gets up your trouser leg when you're standing in the middle of the creek in the rain,
or if you fall in love with your teacher.
And he'll tell you about the McPhees, and his friends, and about the cat whose feet never touch the floor,

   and what happened when a swan's EGG learnt to fly,
   and about the world's only fat butter of a dog,
   and...and...and, well about one or two other things as well...
The first *Niamong* book– nearly 3,000 copies sold.

Lissie Pendle ISBN 978-09806429-3-3 **Ages 8-13**

Lissie Pendle is about trouble. But not trouble with a capital T. It's trouble which just...well, it just happens. Usually with the help of her little brother, or Scratcher and his friends, or just....things.

Lissie is busy, pre-occupied if you like, coping with events and trying to sort out and put in their proper place (ie beside and slightly in awe of her) the various eligible boys of the town. In these endeavours she succeeds quite gloriously, although she's actually the only person who understands this.

In the course of telling us about a number of pretty unusual events, such as the case of the killer koala, or what happened in old-fashioned train toilets, or when she met a lady who inserted capital letters into her conversation, or when there was blood instead of ink in the inkwell, or....well, a pile of other things, we discover an Australia of another time.

When things were clear, including the air, and life was simpler and, yes, funnier.

The second *Niamong* book.

The Search for Quong ISBN 978-0-9806429-2-6 **Ages 7-11**

Quong was a creature of the olden olden days, even before grandmother.

He was a short fellow, or, at least, that's what they said, with long, thin legs and an even longer, thinner tail. His face was fat and wrinkly, and big bushy eyebrows kept out the sun and flies.

At least that's what I think he looked like, though

no—one has actually seen him that I'd believe. Which, of course, was the trouble.

Some people say that there are no such things as quongs, that it's a stupid name, and that if there were any there'd be pink elephants, too.

But those people don't think Father Christmas comes every year, either.

Of course this is all nonsense. There must be quongs and we must find them.

And, if this story's any good, we will.

The third Niamong book.

Ranga Plays Australia ISBN 978-0-646-49692-4 **Ages 12-adult**

It's only four years after the end of World War 2, during which there were no great cricket matches. But now things are getting back to normal: the Australians have thrashed the Poms in England (which is always, and will always be, a good thing), India has played its first Test series in Australia, and 'the Don' has retired.

In a small Bangalore village young Ranganathan Rao is musing about life in general and cricket in particular. Ranga's spinning fingers begin to itch.

Kumar, Ranga's English/Geography/History teacher introduces his pupils to an especially strange word—that he heard an Australian say during the war—and invites them to try to pronounce it and identify its meaning. After many unsuccessful attempts Kumar reveals both the word's pronunciation and meaning, and suggests that everyone might remember this, as one day they might go to Australia.

This starts Ranga thinking. The fourth *Niamong* book. Video

Possum and Python ISBN 978-09806429-4-0   **Ages 7-11**

She lay on a great branch high above the rain forest floor, a splendid creature, shimmering black hair glistening in the starlight.

Above her, on an even higher branch, *another* splendid creature, a mortal enemy.

She didn't know it was there, and it wasn't interested in her, but an extraordinary adventure was about to begin–a tale of surprise, dedication, and, above all, love (which, as we all know, can change the world).

The Day and Night Machine ISBN 978-0-9806429-1-9   **Ages 11-14**

It's Jess's thirteenth birthday. She's been in bed for nearly a year, the result of a car accident that killed her father. Surprisingly, she finds a birthday present from her father, an unusual gift for a girl and one which she, her grandfather, and her mother, puzzle over.

In the course of playing with it she discovers that it has some highly-unexpected properties.

But then, purely by accident, she discovers its most amazing feature.

She wonders how she can use this for the benefit of the world, but is foiled by Miss Sturzen, a villainous redhead, who steals the 'machine' for her own enrichment and evil ends.

When she captures and imprisons Jess, she has a clear run, but Jess is able to circumvent her difficulties and come up with a particularly appropriate counter strategy, aided by a phlegmatic police sergeant and his retinue of puppies.

Miss Sturzen is arrested and taken away, but escapes and returns to wreak mortal revenge on Jess, using a day and night machine. Unfortunately for her, however, things don't quite go to plan.

And then we discover the *real* reason for Jess's father's gift.

It's a good idea to read this before *The Package on the Tram*, but not essential.

The Package on the Tram ISBN 978-0-9806606-7-8 **Ages 11-14**

Sequel to *The Day and Night Machine*

The world's largest dog that vanishes or re-appears out of nowhere, with hairs larger than trees.

Creatures larger than mammoths that can help the tiniest.

A cobweb that changes colour according to whether...

Where Jess can be killed at any moment by anyone she loves, and who love her.

And a decision that leads to a desperate loss.

A mystery story involving a thirteen-year old girl, her unwanted guest, her mother and grandfather, three detectives, a man of two tribes, and a bunch of Labradors with colour-coded collars.

Oh, and a father who may not be really there...

Order online at http://www.lulu.com/spotlight/ianburns or at www.amazon.com or other online retailers.

Twevven in a very dangerous situation ISBN 978-0-9806606-6-1

Ages 4-10

It's a very hot day, so Twevven decides to go to the beach. When he gets there he sees that it's terribly crowded. He then makes a seriously foolish decision. If you ever take a child to the beach you need to read this story first, and discuss what Twevven did wrong and how everything turned out all right in the end.

A must-read if you ever take young children to an ocean beach.

Video

Twevven and the horrible big bigger biggest baby burp ISBN 978-0-9806606-5-4

Ages 4-10

Twevven has forgotten his purse so finds himself 'volunteering' to do something that he's never done before. It is fairly certain that he ends up regretting this.

Video

Order online at http://www.twevven.com

www.ingramcontent.com/pod-product-compliance
Lightning Source LLC
Chambersburg PA
CBHW070548260626
47161CB00002B/541